Storm on the Cathe

Richard Langley

Local Dialect Explained

Perth: Port or Harbour
Cov: Cove
Tol: Tower
Nor: North
Sor: South
Est: East
Wes: West
Math: Manor House
Forn: Forest

Wrea
The "world" on which this story is set. Its prime element is water.

Aiere
One of the three "worlds" linked by magical gates. Aiere is the "air" world.

Erath
The third "world. Its element is earth. It is entirely mountainous.

Kerun Dur
"Acadamy of Light": School for wizards on Aiere.

Die Kashaan Eed
An order of wizards who draw their power from the Void.

Forath
The "hidden isle", home to the Guild of Navigators and Weatherworkers

Notes on pronunciation.

Cathe: Cay-th
Shiranene: Sheer-a-neen
Capradon: Cap-rah-dun
Aiere :   Aye-air-ah
Wrea: Ree-ah
Erath: Air-ath
Teoceromo: Tay-oh-care-oh-moh

Index

Chapter One - The Mageseekers

A scream broke the dawn's stillness and brought back the vivid memory of a morning long ago. Daren turned away to stare grimly out to sea while the chosen children were roused from their sleep, torn from their tearful families and packed into the boats. He turned again to look past the close-packed warehouses and taverns behind the high granite sea defences. Beyond them he could make out the slate roof of the fisherman's cottage where he had spent his early years.

The fourth bollard from the right on the old quay, presently being used to secure the mooring rope of a crank-looking fishing boat, had been his. Daren had been fishing there, shrouded by white mist, when the tall ship had ghosted silently into the bay. He remembered feeling no fear despite the fact that there was not a breath of wind to move a vessel of such size. It moved nonetheless gliding silently between the moored merchant shipping, fishing craft and naval stores ships. He had hardly been able to make it out; just a vague shape in the whiteness. Occasionally dark figures could be seen about the deck and rigging.

Silence. That was what he remembered. Never a call or a shout. No bell sounding to warn other shipping as port regulations required. Even the anchor had slipped into the still water without a splash when the ship came to a halt in the centre of bay.

He'd glimpsed the single boat for just an instant in an opening in the mist. It carried a cargo of cloaked figures being rowed steadily to the shore. Daren had not waited for them to come up. Even at the age of ten he'd known what an ordeal it would have been for his mother. He'd left his neatly coiled fishing line by the front door and trotted down to the main wharf with just the clothes on his back. He'd arrived just in time to tie up the boat for "the gentlemen".

Now Daren was returning on a ship of his own, some twenty years later, with the same gentlemen on the same mission. He had no stomach for what was to follow and his presence was a mere courtesy in any case. The sun was barely above the horizon before today's boat, crammed with youngsters aged between 9 and 18 years of age, left the quay and their sobbing parents behind.

As for the cloaked men, their task had only just begun. Within the hour, the ship had weighed anchor and was already moving on to the next port down the coast. In a few days' time they would start to move inland.

* * * *

A bitter wind swept along the Cathe bringing with it the first taste of winter. On the high ground at the centre of the island of Fain-Arn there was no escaping its chill. The wind flowed unchecked into the grounds of Harton School for Young Ladies where the school's pupils did not welcome it. The young ladies of the school were, at all times of the year, encouraged to get plenty of fresh air. For the most part they now huddled in miserable groups near the wall or under trees. Two figures sat on a bench in the open braving the worst of the cold.

Though both cloaked, neither girl had bothered to raise their hood. On the left sat a girl whose neatly braided blonde hair tried in vain to break free and fall across her face. Of pale complexion, her face was now flushed with the chill of the wind; two red patches underneath fine cheek bones which served to define a face that was delicate, certainly attractive, but also clearly aristocratic. Her bearing was full of self-assurance and her blue eyes shone with animation and intelligence as she leaned forwards in conversation against the wind.

"I heard Madam Hale commended you to the Head, again!"

Her companion, who was similarly dressed, was slightly taller and of more solid build than her friend. Her most striking feature was her hair which was raven black; a real rarity on the island. It was un-braided now and blew wildly in the wind as a visual representation of the spirit and character of its owner. There was a glow about her face which the cold could only in part claim credit for. Close inspection would reveal to a keen observer the same lively intelligence and animation in her eyes. Only the shortest of conversations would suggest the same degree of self-assured confidence as her companion, albeit with less "breeding" behind it.

"It's nothing. I've been doing mathematical problems harder than hers with Father for years." A sigh followed the statement. "At least I've managed to please one of the teachers here. Miss Drake is always criticising my work."

"Don't mind her, Elaine!" A sympathetic hand patted her sleeve. "Everyone finds Miss Drake's lessons tedious."

"It's more than that, Lydia!" Elaine frowned. Miss Drake was very much the bane of her school existence and the strain was beginning to tell. "I know I'm no good at tapestry and I hate her deportment classes. She just doesn't think I should be here at all."

"Your fees get paid the same as everybody else's, don't they? This place would be dire if you weren't here. Anyway, it's the holidays soon."

"True," Elaine agreed. Holidays for her were very much an escape back to normality. Whatever cousin Lydia might say, Elaine was only too aware of how out of place she was amongst the daughters of the island's wealthier population. Lydia herself was the niece of the island's governor but Elaine's mother had married well beneath her station. Only Elaine's tenuous family link to the D'Shan name and her father's surprising ability to pay the school fees ensured her place here.

"Not that I enjoy the holidays much," Lydia continued. "Father is usually far too busy to notice me and Mother expects me to be "on show" when her friends call. It's worse than school and I have no company at all." Although Lydia often felt as her cousin did about the school, its teachers and its rules, it did at least offer variety. At home there was simply no outlet for the restless energy of which her headstrong nature was but a symptom.

"I can't imagine what it's like." Elaine replied. "Holidays are always busy for me. I generally help Father but I expect this time will be different. There's David to think of and

Mother said they've had builders in – the whole place is upside down according to her last letter. They're adding some new-fangled device from Thirnmar to the tower."

"How is David?" Lydia was quite excited by the new addition to her extended family. Elaine was somewhat indifferent. Perhaps when he was old enough to do some of her chores, she thought, there might be a use for him. For now, he took all of her mother's time and robbed Elaine of those precious mornings fishing with her father.

"Not sleeping. It's the noise – or maybe colic."

"Sounds like you'd be better off coming home with me to Wescliffe for the holidays. There's the room next to mine. Mother won't mind and Father will be too busy to notice."

"What, for the whole holidays?"

"Why not? Your parents have a lot on their hands at the moment. We could go riding on the Downs. And of course there's the boathouse..." Lydia let the thought hang in the air. She'd learned a great deal about her cousin this term. Until Elaine had joined Harton School the two cousins had never met or exchanged a word.

"Well, if you think we'd be allowed..." Elaine broke off abruptly as a group of girls approached them.

"Oh look, it's the outcasts!" Mary Newton was the typical product of a wealthy Fain-Arn family. A particular favourite of Miss Drake, she was becoming increasingly bold as the term progressed. "Lydia, I do admire you for taking pity on her but you really should try to spend some time with normal people. You're not going to get far here hanging around with Fishergirl."

"Miss Drake says all her tapestries turn out like fishing nets." Susan Moran clearly felt the need to join in today. "In fact, there's been a bit of a fishy smell about the place since she arrived."

"I'd watch out if I were you Fishergirl," Mary stood over Elaine leaning down slightly in a manner she believed to be intimidating. "Miss Drake doesn't want you here and I'm going to see that she throws you out." A second later she let out a shrill cry of pain as Elaine sprang to her feet and grabbed a fistful of hair. She tugged it down so that Mary's head jerked back.

"Girls!" An imperious sharp voice broke in from behind the group on the path. Instantly Elaine let go, her heart sinking. Miss Drake's timing, as ever, was impeccable. "Conduct yourselves properly!" Elaine hastily pushed Mary away.

"Yes, Miss Drake, sorry Miss Drake," the girls chimed.

"Sheldon!" barked the tutor harshly, spotting Elaine amongst the girls as Mary began to cry theatrically. "I might have known you'd be behind things! Lines after supper tonight. Miss Newton, kindly do not snivel. Young ladies do not snivel. Nor do they lower themselves to the standards of those beneath them." This last comment was delivered with a stern look at Elaine.

Two men had walked up behind Miss Drake. The foremost of the two was a tall, broad-shouldered man. By the tone of his skin and hair he was clearly not a native of any of the islands that made up the Kingdom of Thirnmar. He wore a fine cloak of deep purple. He pulled this tightly about him as if he was unused to the chill wind. The cloak was fastened below his throat with a silver broach of unusual design; an intertwining of woven silver strands which formed shapes that seemed to shift and change if the eye focussed on them for too long. The man's bearing was strong, almost aggressive. His dark eyes darted from one girl to the other; suspicious and accusing without the need for words.

The second stranger wore a similar cloak but this was worn open, revealing robes of royal blue decorated with silver trim beneath. A good few inches shorter than his companion, this man was of slender build with sandy brown hair flecked with the first hints of grey and blue eyes that suggested more local ancestry. This gentleman seemed more relaxed than the other; composed, calm and seemingly indifferent to the blustery wind. His eyes remained fixed at some distant point as if his mind were elsewhere.

The taller of the two now spoke.

"Are these your young ladies, Miss Drake?" The voice rang with an accent none of the girls recognised. Instantly, Miss Drake transformed into her "lady of breeding" personality that the girls knew was reserved only for the rich and important.

"Indeed, all new to the school this year. Mostly from good families I assure you!" The tall stranger dismissed the comment with an irritated wave of the hand.

"Families do not concern me, Miss Drake. Good families do not require my talents. They send their children voluntarily."

"Well, yes," Miss Drake said hastily, unsure where she had gone wrong. "But we do select only the most promising pupils here."

"Perhaps. I shall inspect them later. For now, I must see the older girls."

"Of course." Miss Drake cleared the huddle of girls out of her way with a fierce glare and walked on in the direction of the school building. The tall stranger followed closely behind but the silent man paused for a moment. Seeming to notice the girls for the first time his pale blue eyes travelled to each in turn, catching their gaze for a brief moment in which time seemed almost to skip a beat. It was but a moment, however. Without word or acknowledgement, he moved off to follow Miss Drake. The girls stood silently watching until they were well out of earshot.

"Who were they?" Mary asked. All thought of the quarrel and previous harsh words were gone now.

"I've never seen either before," Susan's voice was a little unsteady. "School Board Officials perhaps? But why do they need to inspect us?"

"Didn't you see the device on his broach?" Lydia asked the group. "He's from the Kerun Dur!"

"What?" Mary was too curious to hide her ignorance.

"He's a Mageseeker. They seek out those with the gift of magic for the academy on Aiera."

"Here? I thought it would be safe!" Elaine's voice was tinged with alarm.

"Safe?" Susan was quick to pick up on Elaine's fear.

"You've never heard of the Mageseekers?" Elaine asked, wondering what these girls did with their time. "They come without warning to every town and village on the island. They take children, killing the parents if need be. Many bear the scars from where they tried to protect their children. If that man picks us we're taken. No choice. It will be years, if ever, before we return. Most children are not heard of again. Even the King has to send his children if they are chosen." Elaine shuddered. The Mageseekers were spoken of often in the taverns near her home; always in hushed tones with half an eye on the door and any strangers present. Elaine had been raised to fear their menace. Their appearances were infrequent – enough so that the children of wealthier families, who generally considered themselves to be above such matters, never heard of them save perhaps as tales told in the nursery.

Elaine had spent much of her formative years in port taverns with her father in the company of sailors who travelled far from the island. It was from them that she had heard tell of the dark sinister men who came to each land and kingdom in the world to take children with the magical gift.

"Can they just take us? From here?" Mary asked, unable to consider the idea that her safety might be in question.

"They can take anyone," Elaine insisted, "from anywhere. You can't hide from them or run from them. The air and sea obeys them. Nor can you resist, for they charm the mind."

The school bell rang summoning the girls to change for tea. The girls huddled together, talking nervously about what the evening might hold. They headed back into school buildings that now seemed much less welcoming and safe.

The food was unusually good that evening. Even this did little to lift the atmosphere of fear and unease that had descended over the entire school. Rumours flew around the tables about how some of the senior girls had been "chosen" earlier and had already left the school.

At the end of the meal the girls were told to remain in their places as the tables were cleared. The tension in the room grew until it became almost unbearable. Neither Lydia nor Elaine were girls who experienced nerves or doubt very often but the atmosphere was infectious. Like everyone else they waited tensely under the Head's grave stare from the end of the room.

"First Year girls will rise quietly and follow me," Miss Drake ordered suddenly from the doorway, breaking the silence. As if in a dream, Lydia and Elaine found themselves filing out of the room with the other girls in their year. There was a deathly silence about the school. Not another pupil was in sight as they walked through the dimly lit corridors to the Art Room.

Normally a friendly area of clutter and paint, the Art Room had been cleared into an empty space. A fire threw light into the room and every lamp had been lit around the walls – an unusual occurrence in a school that watched its costs very closely. The girls, about thirty in all, were lined up on one side of the room. Lydia and Elaine were amongst those furthest from the door, close to the fire whose warmth failed to dispel the chill that had settled upon the group.

"You will stand in silence." Miss Drake's voice was strained. "No girl is to speak unless spoken to."

Four figures entered through the door. The first was the tall stranger from earlier and behind him, the silent one. The two others were dressed similarly to the first but their dark cloaks were thrown back over their shoulders to reveal curved silver swords hanging from jewelled belts; the symbols of their authority. If possible, these new strangers appeared even more sinister than their leader. Their faces were blank and devoid of any emotion and their eyes were dark and cold.

Then an ordeal began which neither girl was ever to forget. Slowly the tall Mageseeker, with the silent one in tow, walked along the row gazing intently at each girl in turn. Some could not meet his gaze. He moved along the line at a steady pace spending exactly the same time appraising each girl before moving on with clockwork precision.

"I had expected to find more!" His harsh voice rang out clearly across the silent room. "Your pupils have less potential than you think, Miss Drake!" Miss Drake cleared her throat nervously, unsure what to say. "This one!" He stopped suddenly in front of one of the youngest girls in the school. "You have the Gift, Child. You will come with us." Peering cautiously up the line, Lydia saw the girl bow her head and, as if in a trance, step out of the line and walk to join the sinister pair by the door.

The effect of this on the rest of the girls was terrible. Several started to cry. Others shrank away from the Mageseeker when he stopped by them only to be pulled back in line by a simple hand gesture, as though they were on an invisible lead.

"Silence!" Miss Drake's voice was brittle and strained, very unlike her usual tone. "Any girl crying shall be given lines. Young ladies do not cry!" Her pronouncement merely quietened the sobs rather than putting a stop to them.

"This one too! You have the Gift yet you are not marked so!" The Mageseeker had stopped again. This time his face betrayed a fiery anger; the first emotion he had shown since entering the room. "Your parents hid you from us?"

"No Sir!" It was more a plea than an answer. Lydia felt her skin chill. The voice was Susan Moran's. The Mageseeker's next pronouncement held a dreadful finality.

"It was foolish. You shall not see them again. Go!" At his command Susan, trembling and tearful, joined the other girl by the door.

As the man came ever closer down the line, Elaine's heart pounded in her chest and her legs became rubbery. At the same time, she felt a curious stubborn anger burn within her. She resented this stranger and his cold voice and lifeless eyes. Thus, when he reached her, she met his gaze despite the terrible fear which threatened to overcome her and made breathing difficult.

"You have the Gift, Child." Like a knife, the words pierced her. Terror exploded ice-cold within her stomach. It was as though her mind became confused then and was suddenly a spectator; watching rather than controlling her actions. Her legs moved of their own accord. Elaine took a step forward out of the line. As she did so a hand clasped her arm in a firm vice-like grip.

Afterwards, Lydia could never explain why. In that instant, when he spoke those words and Elaine took a step forward, she acted on pure instinct. Quickly, she grasped her friend's arm. Lydia dimly heard a shocked gasp from Miss Drake and was aware of the girl to her left shrinking away as if she feared to be too close. Elaine swayed as she was held between the spell and her friend. "Stop that!" The Mageseeker spat the words venomously.

A spark of light exploded about Lydia's hand and a terrific pain shot up her arm, forcing her to release her grip with a cry. Elaine took another step forward and turned towards the door, her head bowed.

"Not this one!" A quiet voice spoke and a second hand came down on Elaine's arm. The silent stranger had spoken for the first time. His voice was softer than the other Mageseeker's but it rang with calm assured authority. The first Mageseeker's face registered further irritation at this second challenge to his choice but the steady gaze of the second man quelled the objection as it formed on his lips.

"Very well." The spell broke suddenly and Elaine dropped painfully to her knees with a gasp. The second man knelt beside her. With surprising gentleness, he helped her stand and step back into line.

"When the time is right you shall seek me out," he told her looking deep into her eyes. "The Kerun Dur is not for you yet, Child, but mine is the harder course to steer. Remember my words!"

Lydia, meanwhile, was trying to meet the gaze of a man twice thwarted. There was malice in his eyes and she could feel her mind growing confused as he took hold of her. The second man turned from Elaine at that point however. He touched the taller man lightly on the arm shaking his head ever so slightly so that only Lydia and her would-be captor saw the gesture. The tall Mageseeker turned from her suddenly in anger and swept quickly down the remainder of the line without picking anyone else.

"Our work is done!" He spoke calmly; his emotions seemingly back under control. "Miss Drake, it has been a pleasure as always." With those words he gestured for the guards to leave the room, which they did ushering the two chosen girls before them. His true feelings were revealed in a final venomous glare at Lydia before he swept out of the room. The once-more silent Mageseeker followed, as ever, a few steps behind without making eye contact with anyone.

A very surreal quiet was left behind which even Miss Drake seemed affected by. She was very pale.

"Girls!" Her voice broke and she had to clear her throat before she could speak again. "Get to your dormitories at once! Lights out in ten minutes."

The Mageseekers' visit cast a shadow over the last two weeks of term that nothing could shake. The teachers from the Head down seemed as deeply affected as the girls under their care. Miss Drake had no inclination to teach, much less criticise, and so Elaine had an easier time of things. Mary Newton suffered an attack of "nerves" which meant she was sent home early. Elaine didn't speak much about the incident with the second Mageseeker.

Lydia didn't press her although she was naturally curious about the whole affair. Instinct told her that Elaine hadn't herself come to terms with it yet. The approaching holiday offered an excuse, perhaps, to place the entire affair at the back of their minds. The immediate future appeared brighter. Elaine's mother had gratefully given permission for Elaine to spend the Harvest holiday with her cousin. Though Lydia was glad of this on a selfish level, she also felt it would afford her the opportunity to keep an eye on her friend.

The three-week holiday was a traditional one granted by the King as reward for the land labourers after the work of getting the harvest in. It provided everyone a chance for some merriment before the nights fully closed in.

So it was that, on a typical autumn afternoon with the light fading, the two girls found themselves sat with their trunks in the back of a cart bumping along the rough track to Wescliffe. The wind had turned to the Wes, driving waves of fine spray and misty rain inland from the Cathe. The girls were soaked to the skin within minutes of setting out. By the time they had bumped and lurched to the coastal track near to Lydia's home, the pair were thoroughly cold and miserable.

Elaine, who was rather more used to such discomfort than her cousin, felt her spirits lift slightly as Wescliffe came into view. Its lights glimmered in the distance through lead-paned windows in welcome. The last stage of the coast track offered a spectacular view of the Cathe. White foam danced on the dark irregular swell in what Elaine knew was exhilarating sailing weather. The murk prevented her spying the distant low line of Thirnmar away to the Wes but occasionally she could see a ship scudding along under a fair press of sail, presumably going to Krann Bay she thought. The vessel was too far out to be heading for Fain-Arn's main port of Perth Cathe to their Sor.

Lydia was far too cold to care about the view, which to her was both familiar and dull. Her thoughts were fixed on dry clothes and a warm bath. She was actually looking forward to arriving home! That, Lydia sniffed miserably to herself, had to be a first.

The cart finally lurched through a gate and into the grounds of Wescliffe where it pulled up, with a final attempt to unseat the passengers, outside the front of the house. The door opened and light spilled out to greet them as the driver helped the girls down from their perch. They were stiff and sore from the journey but welcoming arms drew them in out of the rain whilst male servants handled the trunks.

"Miss Lydia, Miss Elaine! You're wet through! To your rooms at once. You'll catch your deaths!" The D'Shan's housekeeper was a woman of about forty-five years of age who had an authority that Miss Drake could never hope to have, being born of over twenty-five years of experience. Like a mother hen with her brood she ushered the girls up the stairs. "Now get out of those wet clothes and dry yourselves! There are clothes laid out for you on the beds. Cook has some food for you, which I'll have brought up in a moment. Make yourself at home, Miss Elaine. If you need anything you have but to ask one of the maids." Lydia disappeared quickly into her room leaving Elaine to explore her room alone.

Chapter Two – Wescliffe

Elaine found herself in a world alien to her. The bedroom, which was the humblest guest room at Wescliffe, was five times the size of her small room at home. A fire blazed in the grate at the far end of the room near to which was a large towel and a comfortable looking armchair. Within seconds Elaine was sitting deep in the armchair snuggled inside the towel. The high back seemed to catch the fire's warmth. It enveloped her in it, banishing the cold and damp as well as her cares. As she relaxed, Elaine looked about her surroundings.

The floor was polished boards but several faded rugs covered large areas making the place seem more homely. There was a huge wardrobe, a writing table near to the window and a small bedside table with an oil lamp. The wood furniture around the room was dark but polished to a sheen that had a reddish tinge in the firelight. Elaine's gaze was inevitably drawn to the inviting double bed, complete with plump pillows and crisp embroidered linen. This room alone represented more wealth than the entire contents of her home, Elaine realised. A maid knocked and entered the room.

"Miss Elaine, I've left your food next door. Is everything to your liking?"

"Oh yes!" Elaine replied. "It's lovely. Thank you." The maid smiled and excused herself. Reluctantly Elaine lifted herself out of the armchair. The nightshirt laid out for her was little different from the one she normally wore – except it was made out of silk rather than linen. The fine material was almost weightless and was possibly the most comfortable garment she had ever worn. Feeling rather like a princess, she went onto the landing and knocked at Lydia's door.

"Come in!" Lydia was dressed in an identical nightshirt lounging on the bed with a tray in front of her. Her room was a mirror image of Elaine's in layout but was carpeted and had more pictures on the wall. "Tuck in. Cook always spoils me when I come home!"

Elaine ate her food cross-legged on the floor near to the fire. The thought of spilling anything on the expensive bedding was more than she could bear - she knew all too well the work involved in washing sheets as it was one of her chores at home. In any case, she enjoyed the heat on her face. The only fire at home was in the kitchen and Elaine always sat close to it at meal times. Tonight Elaine ate in silence listening to Lydia's chatter.

The transformation was amazing she thought. Lydia at school was a far more nervous and hesitant character. One of the reasons the girls had become close friends was that Lydia did not mix well with the other pupils at the school. Here she was transformed into a confident wealthy young lady secure in her own home. She was waited on by servants who addressed her as "Miss" rather than "D'Shan". Lydia was full of plans but Elaine was too tired to think ahead this night. She was content to revel in the warmth of the fire and feel the pleasant sensation of nourishing food inside her.

After a while, Elaine excused herself and padded back to her own room. The fire had almost died down and despite the full bucket of coal provided for her use she left it to go out. She was used to a cold room and a draught from the crack in her window. A final surprise awaited her in bed in the form of a hot brick wrapped in a towel. Amazed at the trouble taken on her behalf, Elaine settled into a bed that redefined comfort. She fell quickly into a deep and refreshing sleep.

As the household at Wescliffe was settling down for a quiet night, another household was being disturbed. A cloaked rider, braving the cold and damp, arrived at the residence of Fain-Arn's Governor at the gallop.

The rider sprang from his horse then ran to the door and hammered upon it, muttering curses under his breath as the servants hurried to answer his summons. The gentleman who opened the door to him had served as butler at Math Calran for just over forty years.

"May I help you Sir?" The rain was heavy and the night dark so he raised his lamp to better see the nocturnal guest.

"Indeed you may. I wish to see my father."

"Master Tristan?" The old man's voice quavered and the lamp trembled.

"Of course. Did you think, or hope, that I had left for good?"

"You are not welcome here!" The door began to close but suddenly it sprang inward, trapping the servant behind it and slamming him against the wall. The lamp tumbled to the floor, shattered and went out.

"Then an unwelcome guest I shall be!" Tristan replied shortly and strode into the building. A flick of his hand slammed the door shut against the night and allowed the servant to slump to the floor where blood now mingled with the lamp oil.

Lord Galvin D'Shan was in the library. He looked up as the door opened suddenly without warning and met a pair of eyes as strong and unyielding as his own. Gently he closed the book he had been reading.

"Father." Tristan stepped into the room yet his face, like the rest of him, remained partially hidden within a cloak that appeared to generate a shadow all of its own.

"Tristan. You should not look for welcome here. You left under a shadow of your own making. Your time since has been spent in darkness of a worse sort, if I hear aright."

"You were always well informed, Father," Tristan replied evenly. "You cast me out and I have been forced to find a path for myself. I have learned much and now I have decided to return."

"Why? There is nothing for one of your kind here."

"There is *everything* for me here!" Tristan's voice rang with anger. "Am I not of your line? The Governorship of this island is mine to claim. I feel the time is close when I shall do so."

"Indeed?" The Governor rose to his feet slowly, wincing slightly as he did so.

"Age lies heavy upon you, Father."

"Not so heavy as you would wish, Son." Galvin's eyes met those of the son he had disowned with a mixture of sorrow and resolute anger. "Your claim to my title was removed when you left. The King would not recognise you; nor would he ever tolerate your presence here. As your father, I give you leave to go – but be warned that the sentence of banishment is upon you. If your face is seen again within the Kingdom you will suffer for it." Tristan took a swift step forward, his hands raised to strike. "NO!" The Governor of Fain-Arn raised his walking stick to protect himself with a shout and Tristan recoiled.

"May you rot in eternal suffering," the younger man hissed venomously as he backed away. "Very well, Father, you need time to think. I say this to you. I have returned and I am here to stay. If you attempt to thwart me, if you set yourself against my will, then you shall pay a high price indeed. I will bring sorrow to you and any who oppose me. The King cannot aid you. There is no-one in the entire Kingdom with the power to set themselves against me. I shall allow you a few days to consider this. Good night – and take care until next we meet." He spun about and left the house, leaving his father to discover the corpse in his front hall.

Sunlight spilled through the window onto Elaine's face waking her from a world of dreams into a reality that had a dreamlike quality of its own. Warm water was provided for her to wash. A maid insisted on unpacking her trunk and laying out clothes for her. Elaine had packed the very best clothes she owned but even her best dress would have looked plain next to the dress Lydia was wearing at breakfast.

The girls dined in the old nursery; a room vast in proportions and littered with the toys of Lydia's childhood.

"Meals with my parents are incredibly tedious," Lydia explained. "Cook usually lets me eat meals alone. Naturally, we'll have to put in an appearance this evening. It's your first day here and even Father will make an effort since you're a guest. After that we'll be mostly free unless they have any visitors. That doesn't happen too often; we're a bit remote here you see." Elaine grinned.

"Compared to TolSor, this isn't remote! We're the only house for miles, apart from the fire towers but they're abandoned now."

"What are fire towers?" Lydia asked with her mouth full of toast (something which would have incurred Miss Drake's wrath had she been at school).

"I'm not sure. They're beacon towers really, a bit like ours but smaller. Strange thing is that they run inland; they don't follow the coastline at all. Father says they're an old warning system from when the islands were under attack by Wheldor's fleet."

"That's a few years ago," Lydia commented absently looking out of the window. "What are we going to do today then?" We can't stay in too long. Mother will have us on show for her friends and we do enough tapestry at school thank you very much! I'd like to go riding!"

"That sounds good although I'd have to change." Elaine shuddered. "There's no way I'm riding side-saddle! Dangerous, that. I'd like a look at your boathouse too." Lydia laughed.

"We can do that first if you like. I know you'll pester me until we do!" Elaine sniffed.

"I wasn't pestering; I was just saying!"

An hour later the pair had dressed more casually. Lydia wore her riding dress with a cloak. Elaine chose her newest "working" clothes which comprised of several layers of warm woollen garments, knitted by her mother, with fresh canvas trousers to keep out the wet. A borrowed cloak from Lydia completed the outfit. The two girls raced down the steep slippery path from Wescliffe to the small cov at the foot of the cliffs. Nestled at the head of the bay was a squat grey stone boathouse with a short slipway descending to the sea. Elaine narrowly won the race but had to wait for Lydia to fumble with the keys and battle the rusty lock.

They entered the back door which opened onto a wooden gantry around the inside of the building. The only light came through the open door and two moss-encrusted skylights in the roof. Elaine's first impression was that they were somewhere they did not belong. The place had clearly been undisturbed for years judging by the cobwebs and a unique smell of damp wood, salt and seaweed. The gantry put them at deck level of a yacht which was mostly hidden under a shroud of filthy canvas.

"Heavens!" Elaine exclaimed. In places, the covers had slipped and a sleek wooden hull could be glimpsed beneath. Lydia was nervous.

"I'm not really supposed to come down here."

"Oh, who's going to know?" Elaine was moving further along the gantry while Lydia remained by the door. "This boat hasn't been out in a long while," she continued thoughtfully, reaching out to touch an area of exposed wood.

"I don't think it has," Lydia agreed. "Father's never used it. He's not interested in boats; doesn't have the time. Here, what are you doing?"

"Just having a peek!" Elaine tugged at the tarpaulin and loosened it further. "Oh my, what a beauty!" She ran her hands gently along the polished hull. "Look at these lines! This was built for speed. And that windlass back there, I bet it's for launching her. All nicely greased....." her voice trailed off.

"No, Elaine! Don't even think it. We can't. Father would kill me!"

"Well, the wind's still in the Wes," Elaine said. "You'd need an offshore breeze to get out of this bay, though getting back in would be tricky I grant you. You'd have to time it very well. Could be done though!"

"Not without permission!" Lydia insisted.

"Well, when the wind's right ask for it?" Elaine suggested. "Come on Lydia, think of the fun! Between us we could sail her easily. We'd have a great run down the Cathe and back. Freedom! I've missed the sea so much at that forsaken school of ours!"

"Well we can't do anything today," Lydia said firmly, putting off the decision. "And I've missed riding as much as you've missed sailing. Let's lock up and go to the stables."

By the time the light of day had dipped towards the horizon and the lamps were being lit at Wescliffe, the girls were exhausted. They had spent the day riding across the downs Est of Wescliffe. Their exploration had taken them many miles over the rolling expanse of sheep and cattle-cropped grass, sparse scrub and gorse bushes. Hidden amongst the latter were sheltered dells, hidden from sight and out of the wind.

It was in one of these that the girls had rested the horses and eaten their lunch, gazing up at the white clouds scudding across the grey autumn sky. Distant birdsong was punctuated by the occasional cry of gulls blown inland on yesterday's gusty wind. Out of the wind the day was crisp, rather than bitterly cold. The ride had warmed them enough to be comfortable in their sheltered spot. The friends chatted and laughed while the horses took their ease close by.

The afternoon was spent in easy exploration, accompanied by occasional bursts of exhilarating speed when the terrain became even enough to allow the horses to show what they could do. Lydia was by far the most accomplished rider of the two but Elaine compensated by applying reckless stubborn determination. Allied with a horse of a similar nature, this allowed her to keep up with her cousin.

They spied a couple of distant croft houses, squat and solid in the unforgiving landscape, but they didn't see another person anywhere. It was as though the land had been loaned to them alone for a short while and was theirs to enjoy.

As evening drew in both girls, who had not ridden for a while, were beginning to feel a hint of the pain that was to come. The sheer freedom and space had lifted their spirits. A certain amount of discomfort was a small price to pay. Lydia, who was much fairer than her cousin, had a healthy glow in her cheeks. Elaine was much more used to spending time outdoors, generally in rain or high wind since that was when her father needed her most. Like Lydia, she felt the weight of school lift away and the welcome prospect of three weeks of such freedom stretched before her. The "glow" was present but affected her spirit rather than her complexion as she prepared herself for the evening meal.

Looking at the reflection in the mirror, Elaine could not help but be acutely aware of how out of place she was here. Her best dress was fine for local occasions but even here in the bedroom it looked drab. She had no doubt that the luxurious dining room at Wescliffe would not improve the impression. There was nothing to be done however so she went to see Lydia (who was always late) to hurry her along.

"You're looking nice!" the compliment startled Elaine.

"This dress is awful!" she objected. Not envious by nature, Elaine felt a sudden desire to be able to dress as well as Lydia. Her cousin had a huge wardrobe to choose from and she had made full use of it this evening. She was wearing a dress of royal blue silk, which set off her hair and eyes. A silver chain about her neck supported a droplet shaped diamond. "Yours on the other hand, I mean you look stunning Lydia!" Lydia shrugged.

"I like to make the effort once in a while, though I'd never admit it to Miss Drake! She'd have me married off in an instant!"

"Why aren't you interested in marriage, Lydia?" Elaine asked the question purely out of curiosity. The issue simply wasn't relevant to her but Lydia's options on that side of things were virtually unlimited. She could attend balls on Thirnmar – she was always being invited – and meet the wealthiest and best of Thirnmar's eligible men. Elaine had no doubt that offers of marriage would not be hard to come by for her friend.

"I'm too young," Lydia replied. "Look, Elaine, it's different for you. You have TolSor. You help your father work the tower and you sail. If you were to marry that won't change much, except when you have babies obviously." She sighed.

"My freedom, such as it is, ends the minute that some man puts an engagement ring on my finger. I'd have to stay in, receive guests, play music, do tapestry. I'd have to gossip like some mindless fool about what Miss So-and-so wore last week and the shocking thing Mr Whatsisname said to the magistrate's wife! Urgh! I'm sorry Elaine but you simply have no idea how tedious life can be here. The truth is, I'm afraid if that happens to me I'll lose my mind. I hate the thought of it, truly I do. I can at least put things off while I'm at school. Mother and Father both see the value of school. The trouble is they only see it as a way of making me more marriable!"

"We'd still be friends though. We can keep in touch. Just marry a man who's away a lot!" Elaine's concern brought a smile to Lydia's face.

"But of course! I'm thinking along the lines of someone in the navy. Well connected, naturally. They're often quite handsome and, most importantly, not at home much!"

"I suppose." Elaine considered the idea. "The officer's uniforms are quite nice, especially the admirals; lots of gold!" Lydia shook her head.

"Too old! I need a Captain, a young Captain, from a good family. That will do me. But not yet! Now, about your dress?"

"Lost cause I'm afraid."

"I don't think so. I'd lend you one of mine but..."

"I know." Not only were the two girls different in colouring, but also their height and build were sufficiently different to rule that idea out. What looked great on Lydia would look terrible on Elaine.

"What you need is to dress it up a bit." Lydia rummaged in her wardrobe and produced a length of silk that was a slightly deeper shade than Elaine's berry coloured dress. "Tie this around your waist," she said. A few more moments rummaging produced some ribbon of the same colour. "Now, if you tie your hair back with this... there! Better?" It was an improvement Elaine had to admit. It added much needed style to a plain dress.

"Thank you, Lydia."

"Hey, you help me with my maths prep, remember?" A gong sounded downstairs. "Right. Try to relax Elaine you are family after all."

The meal was an ordeal for Elaine who hated being "on show". However, Lydia's parents made an effort to make polite conversation afterwards and Elaine at least felt that she had not disgraced herself or shamed her parents. Lydia offered moral support throughout, not least with navigating the large amount of cutlery that appeared to be necessary. Over drink, after the dessert, Lydia found herself on the receiving end of a very detailed account of a wealthy young man who had visited a family friend in Woolton a few days previously. He had called at Wescliffe only a day before the girls' arrival.

"Lucky we weren't here," Elaine said at this point, thinking of her earlier conversation with Lydia. The description stopped abruptly and both of Lydia's parents looked sharply at her. Lydia's eyes widened in horror. Elaine thought very quickly. "Miss Drake says that young ladies of good standing do not receive gentlemen callers at home," Elaine explained smoothly. "It was improper of him to call and it would have been *most* embarrassing to have to make excuses. Miss Drake is very knowledgeable about such things isn't she Lydia?" This question was delivered in such an innocent tone that Lydia almost spilled her drink.

"Yes," she managed to reply.

"She says it is very important for young ladies of Lydia's standing to observe the correct etiquette. Young men these days can be quite inconsiderate of such things."

"Well, certainly that is the case!" Mrs D'Shan agreed, quite surprised. "I shall most certainly turn him away if he calls again."

"You are terrible!" Lydia exclaimed afterwards amidst a fit of giggles. They had escaped to the nursery.

"You nearly gave the game away!" Elaine scolded. "You must learn to control yourself! Young ladies do not spill their drinks. Nor do they accept gentlemen callers!" Elaine had perfected her "Miss Drake voice" with much practice.

"Young men can be *so* inconsiderate!" Lydia's version was almost as good. "Oh Elaine, thank you! I doubt Mother will accept gentlemen callers for a month now!"

"No problem, it was a pleasure." Elaine's tone changed slightly as it did when she was contemplating something cunning. "Of course, you could return the favour you know."

"How?" Lydia was suddenly cautious.

"Well, the wind's backing to the Nor-Est. You could ask your father about the boat."

"I'm not sure..."

"Come on, Lydia! I saved you from that young man, didn't I? I bet your mother was going to invite him over and you would have had to go out walking with him."

"All right!" Lydia could tell when she was defeated. "I'll speak to Father tomorrow."

"He seems to be in a good mood tonight," Elaine suggested, pushing her luck.

"You don't give up, do you?"

"Family trait."

Thomas D'Shan's study was a room designed to impress the visitor with the importance of its owner. The furniture was of the highest quality. A huge oak desk, formerly from a warship, dominated the end of the room nearest to the fire. Papers and books were stored about the room interspersed with small artistic objects such as a model warship and a chart of the waters around Fain-Arn.

Curiously, Lydia could not recall entering it before. Her father was seated behind the desk working on the huge Revenue Ledger in which was recorded the entire tax records and expenses for the island. He looked up in some surprise and a little irritation, a finger firmly poised over the column on which he was working.

"Yes, Child?"

"Father, I, that is, Elaine and I, want to ask you something."

"Very well. I am a little busy here," he replied.

"Well, as you know Elaine is a very good sailor, much better than I am... although I'm pretty good," she added hastily. "Well, what we were wondering was..."

"Hmm?" Mr D'Shan's interest had wandered back to the ledger.

"... whether we might take the boat out. Elaine is very sensible. We'd only go if it was safe and we'll take good care."

"I see." Mr D'Shan made a small mark in the margin noting that he had gone wrong somewhere. He would have to rework the figures for the naval dockyard at Perth Cathe to get the figures to balance. "Well?" He looked up, having lost the thread of the conversation utterly.

"Can we then?" Lydia asked, seeing the opportunity and exploiting it.

"What? Oh, yes of course. Very well."

"Thank you, Father!" Lydia surprised both of them by giving him a kiss on the cheek.

"Mind the ink dear!" he exclaimed mildly. "It has to be past your bedtime Child. Off you go!"

"Of course, Father, good night." Lydia skipped out of the door and ran upstairs to give Elaine the good news. She left her father wondering what he had just agreed to.

"Ah well," he murmured to himself. If it kept the girls out of mischief it couldn't be all that bad, could it? And he needed peace to get these figures right. Best part of tomorrow that was going to take if he was any judge. Thomas D'Shan sighed, closed the ledger and dowsed the lamp. He considered mentioning the conversation with Lydia to his wife. She could find out... but no. Lydia's temper was at least fifty per cent inherited from her mother. Best not to mention it. With a bit of luck, nothing bad would come of it.

Chapter Three - Perth Cathe

Elaine's first action on awakening the following morning was to rush to the window. The Cathe's weather patterns befuddled even the most ancient of seafarers. Although she had seen promising signs yesterday there was no guarantee…but yes! The wind was brisk, steady and just Nor of Est. A regular swell sparkled in the distance and there was a slight sea haze that was sure to lift soon. It couldn't be better. Elaine banged on the wall to wake Lydia and dressed herself for the day's adventure.

Over a hasty breakfast the girls made their plans. Lydia was to secure some food from cook, who was both generous and discreet. At the same time, Elaine would go down to the boathouse and make ready.

"Don't worry!" she assured Lydia. "I'll wait for you to come down before I launch her!"

It was quite dark in the boathouse but Elaine resisted the temptation to open the main doors just yet. Carefully, she released the ties and hauled the heavy tarpaulin covers out of the way. It was no small job but she was not unused to such things having been around working boats all her life. By the time Lydia arrived, laden with the spoils of a pillaged larder, the covers were off and the sails had been brought up out of their storage lockers.

"You've been busy!"

"Don't want to waste the wind," Elaine explained a little breathlessly.

"Well, have a drink. You're red as anything."

"In a minute." Elaine scrambled off the boat and darted along the gantry towards the front of the boathouse. "Ready?" Lydia nodded. Elaine reached up to a heavy counterweight on a chain and hauled sharply downwards. The boathouse doors swung open and daylight flooded in to reveal the boat in all its glory.

The lines of the hull were sleek and fine. The woodwork fairly glowed in the sunlight, the varnish being undimmed by water or exposure to the light. The boat's name was mounted on the bows and stern in slightly faded brass letters: SKYLARK. "Let's get her in the water first. Shouldn't be too difficult!"

"Are you sure about this?" Lydia was having a sudden attack of nerves. Whilst it was true that this boat had lain untouched in the boathouse for years, it was clearly very expensive. To Elaine it was just another boat, albeit a particularly fine one. They were not things to be nervous of.

"You'd better jump aboard now, unless you want to swim out after I've launched her!" Elaine called as she moved towards the steps running down to the windlass at the back of the boathouse. The mechanism seemed simple enough. A large hammer hung on a hook next to it. Elaine hefted the hammer in her hands, testing the weight as she looked up at Lydia's face peering down at her from the stern. "Better move over to the port side," she advised, "and hold on tight!" Taking careful aim, she swung the hammer hard against a wooden pin knocking it cleanly out. For a split second nothing happened. Then there was a groan from beneath the boat as if the house was finding it painful to release the prize it had held safe for so long.

SKYLARK shuddered then began to move smoothly towards the door. Elaine dropped the hammer and threw herself at the rickety staircase up to the gantry. By the time she got to the top, the boathouse was echoing to the rattle of chain links pouring in a glistening molten stream from the pit below the windlass. SKYLARK was picking up speed and the bows were already outside the door.

Sprinting hard, Elaine pounded to the end of the gantry, vaulted the rail and took a flying leap onto the deck. She landed gracefully as the SKYLARK slipped outside and made the short journey down the slipway. The boat hit the water evenly, raising a veil of spray around her.

The girls yelled in wild delight as they drifted gently to a stop a few feet from the end of the slipway. Elaine quickly tossed a light anchor over the bow to hold them steady in the cov, pointing out to sea. She immediately busied herself with raising the mast, which at present rested along the boat's length on cradles. Lydia watched the expert at work and lent a hand or two when told to. Otherwise, she kept out of the way until the tricky business was complete.

They rested for a few minutes, drinking some water and feeling very pleased with themselves. Elaine, however, was unable to just sit quietly for long. Lovely though SKYLARK was, she was not yet all she could be. New cream sails waited to be set and the boat tugged impatiently at her mooring. She seemed to be eagerly straining towards open water at the mouth of the cov.

"Do you want to steer or set the sails?" Elaine asked.

"It's been a while since I've done this," Lydia replied. "You had better get the sails up. I can keep her headed out of the bay until you get back here."

"Just listen out," Elaine reminded her cousin with a grin. "And relax! It's a great day to be on the water. Tell you what; we'll go out under the jib. We'll get the mainsail up once we're underway. I can come back and give you a hand if you need me!" With that she was gone, scrambling forward. Shortly afterwards the jib climbed smoothly skywards and SKYLARK's tugging at her moorings became more purposeful. On cue, Lydia released the catch attaching the stern to the boathouse windlass and tossed out a buoy in order that the chain might be recovered later. As SKYLARK slipped forwards, Elaine snatched the anchor out of the shale and hauled it back up on deck. By the time it was secured, SKYLARK was picking up the first of the swell.

Lydia gave Elaine the thumbs up and so, making the most of what little shelter remained of the land, Elaine set the mainsail. She secured everything as it should be before heading aft to join Lydia at the tiller.

Elaine found her cousin somewhere between delight and abject terror. Lydia liked to sail as much as her cousin but circumstances rarely permitted it. When she did sail it was in small single-sailed craft. Never had she taken a boat this big out to sea. SKYLARK's sails were drawing well but she had the feel of a thoroughbred and Lydia was not feeling at all confident in her ability to meet the challenge. It was with some relief that she handed over to the more experienced sailor.

The truth of the matter, however, was that SKYLARK was very unlike the lugger Elaine sailed occasionally with her father on fishing trips. Where the lugger might be a sturdy beast of burden, SKYLARK would be a racehorse. Elaine felt a wild elation within her as she began to get the measure of the boat. The tiller was responsive and the wind steady. Things could not be better. Once they were well clear of land, Elaine brought SKYLARK round to point Sor, heading along the Cathe parallel to the coast. This brought the wind to just aft of their beam. Their sleek little craft fairly sprang forward with a ferocity that was both wonderful and terrifying at once. The sails pressed SKYLARK far over onto her side and before long Lydia and Elaine were sat on the windward beam, leaning as far out as they dared.

Salt spray whipped about them as the sea flew by a short distance below. Their hair flew wildly about their faces. It felt as though they were part of the very sea itself, borne along by a force both powerful and nurturing. Dangerous though the Cathe could be, today it was their friend and they were at one with it.

Time and the shoreline slipped by. After a while, Lydia took a turn at the tiller and felt the trembling power of rushing water beneath her fingers. Elaine was content to relax although she kept half an eye on Lydia and the set of the sails. Perth Cathe, situated to the Nor of a wide bay, presented Elaine with something of a problem when it came into sight some two and a half hours later. It was impossible to reach a decent mooring straight away. They headed into the bay on a Sor-Est heading, virtually a beam reach, but their eventual destination lay right into the wind. Not wanting to risk tacking amidst heavy traffic, Elaine opted to continue on towards the centre of the bay before bringing SKYLARK as close to the wind as she would come (which was pretty close) and fetching a reasonable mooring in one go.

This plan went very well until they neared a likely looking buoy. Lydia had another attack of the jitters.

"I can't steer her here!" she objected. "There are too many other boats about. What if I hit one?" Elaine sighed.

"Well, you'll have to lower the sails then. Wait 'till I say. Don't worry too much about how they come down, just get them down!" As SKYLARK came up into the wind, her sails shivering, Elaine gave Lydia the signal. The mainsail came down with a run unravelling the halliard in the process and smothering the deck (and Lydia) in a mass of crumpled canvas. Elaine's ears burned as she heard a raucous laugh from nearby but she had to ignore it. Abandoning the tiller, she moved forward and picked up the mooring just as SKYLARK lost way and began to slip back on the tide.

Only then could she rescue a rather shame-faced Lydia and assess the damage. It could have been a lot worse, she thought. The sail had received a bit of a dunk in the filthy water of the port and would need some serious attention before returning to creamy white. This horrified Lydia but such things happened and Elaine was more concerned with the rigging.

"I'd better do this now," she said. "We don't want to be worrying about it when we're trying to set sail for home. You can get the sails stowed properly and tidy up a bit."

"Yes Captain!" Lydia's attempt at humour was so down-hearted Elaine had to grin.

"Cheer up. It's fine. Won't take a minute, Lydia, then we can go ashore. I've done that a few times myself you know!"

"Really?" Lydia brightened slightly.

"Sure," lied Elaine. "It's no problem. Now, I'll be back down in a minute."

The view from the top of the mast was so fascinating that "a minute" turned into ten. Elaine had a view of the entire harbour from the merchant wharves, through the general shipping to the navel yards. Three tall ships were in port loading with wool, wood and ale. These were the three main exports off the island. The naval repair yard was empty but for two small supply vessels. Out in the centre of the bay a small frigate was swinging heavily at its anchor. It seemed to be the centre of remarkable activity with boats plying from it to the main waterfront and back again.

The smells of the port were all familiar to her: tar, rope, fish, seaweed and that curious salty shoreline smell which carries out to sea and is so welcome to sailors returning from a long voyage. The sounds of the port were distinct to her ears, though to Lydia they mingled into a general cacophony: the chanting and stamping of men working to a rhythm, shouts of men calling from one ship to another seeking information from others of their cargo, a fair bit of cursing as the waters were busy and smaller craft often got in each other's' way, singing and music from the taverns on the waterfront, laughter from a party of sailors who had already had a few drinks too many.

This was a different world to Wescliffe but it was Elaine's world. This was where her father and she brought their catch on those rare precious occasions when they were able to put out of CovTol and fish.

"Are you staying up there all day?" Lydia's call broke in upon her thoughts and brought her back into the here and now.

"All fixed, I'll be right down." Moments later her feet landed lightly on the deck. A boat was bumping alongside them although Lydia had dropped fenders over the side to protect the polished woodwork.

"Going ashore?" By the tattoos and the scars Elaine took the man for an ex-navy type. A healthy man could make a fair living rowing people ashore and this man looked like he'd think nothing of rowing through a hurricane. However, Elaine was not a newcomer to the port and she decided to set terms as her father had instructed her. "*There are plenty of folks that will part a fool from their money*," was her father's oft-quoted maxim when it came to dealings in Perth Cathe.

"We are," she replied. "A penny each for the round trip; we'll be leaving before the tide turns again this afternoon. We pay half now and half on return to the boat." The man looked up at her and considered the offer.

"As you say, Miss. Nice boat you have there. Very trim."

"Will it be alright here?" Elaine asked.

"I should think so Miss," the man replied in some surprise, nodding towards the stern. Following his gaze, Elaine saw that Lydia had shipped a short staff from which an ensign fluttered. It bore the D'Shan coat of arms.

"I found it in a little locker under the counter," Lydia explained. "Shall we?" The port fascinated Lydia as their guide rowed them through the throng towards the waterfront. This was a new world to her. Seeing her expression, the man slowed his pace slightly and pointed out anything he thought might be of interest.

"That there, Miss, is the Shiranene," he said, gesturing to a small sleek-looking schooner moored by a merchant jetty. "Just in today she is, quite the talk of the town. First time she's put in here; doesn't usually bother with us! Mostly she sails to Thirnmar. Now, you notice her ensign on the stern there?"

"The black and yellow one?" Lydia enquired. "I've seen that before somewhere, I think."

"Not too often!" the man replied. "She's from Wheldor. We don't see many of their ships, unless they get caught in the Cathe during a gale of course! Then they put in anywhere." Wheldor, the girls knew, was the large island kingdom far off to the Est. There was a long history of war between their own kingdom and Wheldor but these days they traded peacefully. There was even talk of marriage between the two royal families.

"What about the frigate?" Elaine asked.

"HMS Hunter," their guide replied. "42 guns, Captain Etheridge. Came in with the tide this morning. Must be on leave I reckon; more than half the crew's ashore. There's bound to be trouble at chucking-out time. You ladies would do well to keep away from the navy taverns, if you'll pardon the advice."

"It's alright," Elaine told him. "I've been here before with my father. I'm Daniel Sheldon's daughter."

"TolSor?"

"That's right."

"Ah, best if I don't mention the little trouble you had with your mainsail then?" he grinned mischievously.

"That was my fault," Lydia admitted hastily, not wanting to embarrass Elaine.

"You're not the first, Miss," he assured her. "You reshipped that halliard smartly, Miss Sheldon. Not many your age can do that. Truly born to the sea you are and a credit to your father! Now," this as the boat came up alongside the waterfront, "if you're after the tide you'll want to meet me back here no later than three hours. I guess from that flag of yours you'll be heading back up the coast. Wind's going to hold and shift a couple of points to the Wes, so that won't be a problem, but the light will be fading by the time you get back."

"Thank you," Elaine said. "We won't be late."

For a time, the two girls wandered where their curiosity took them. As the main port for the island, Perth Cathe attracted a fair mixture of people. The shops and stalls reflected this so for a while the pair lost themselves amidst the sights, smells and sounds.

The street performers particularly fascinated Lydia as she'd not come across them before. Begging was rather frowned upon on the island but if someone was willing to entertain, the islanders were generous enough in their charity. Some of the performers had pets that had been trained to perform simple tricks. There were tumblers and mime artists. One of the latter had the girls in stitches. Slapstick comedy was always a crowd-puller and this man had the comic timing of a genius.

Elaine found herself drawn to the sound of a wooden flute which she eventually located at the edge of the market. The quality of the sound was wonderfully clear and mellow, not at all shrill as some flutes she had heard. The tune was hauntingly mournful. It had a hypnotic quality that seemed to transport her far across the sea to some distant place. Beside the musician was laid out a selection of flutes. Elaine picked one up and examined it.

The wood was hand-carved with loving care. A pattern of curling waves ran up each side and the mouthpiece was shaped like a shell. The musician stopped playing suddenly.

"You like?" His voice had a lilting quality and accent, not unlike the music he had been playing.

"It's very beautiful," Elaine replied honestly. "But I can't afford this I'm afraid. I liked the music you were playing. Do you make the flutes yourself?"

"With my own hands I do." The man bobbed his head. "Tell me Child, what did you hear when I was playing?" Elaine gently replaced the flute and considered the question for a moment.

"I'm not sure. I found myself thinking about a calm sea under moonlight. I felt as though the music came from far away. I…. can't quite explain it."

"No need! You hear well Child. Here, take it." He picked up the flute and offered it.

"No! I can't." Elaine shook her head.

"Yes! It is a gift. You see? There is no price. My flutes are not for sale. You may have it." The man scrambled nimbly to his feet. Even then his head scarcely came to Elaine's waist. The cloak he was wearing fell away to reveal pale blue skin and bright aqua coloured eyes. "It is good luck to accept my gift. You know?"

"Yes, I accept," Elaine said, suddenly serious. "Thank you."

"You have a good ear for music." The man bowed. "And you are very pretty."

"Thank you," Elaine repeated, feeling herself blush slightly.

"May good fortune be with you."

"Fair winds and safe return." Elaine gave the reply without thinking, the memory of it returning from some distant time when she was very young. Satisfied, the man settled down again and returned to his music. Elaine to walked back into the thick of the market. The haunting music followed her as she went. She found Lydia looking at a fabric stall.

"What's that?" Lydia asked immediately.

"A flute. That man gave it to me. Well, not a man actually."

"Oh?" Lydia took the flute and examined it. "Is this…?"

"Yes, a gift from a Sea Sprite. He wished me good fortune. I thought they were just sea-stories."

"Sprites? No! They're actually quite common; more so on Thirnmar than here. Mother knew one once when she was a girl. She said he was quite charming. They are very well mannered, you know, though they can be quite flirtatious. I do believe Mother was rather taken with him!"

"I can imagine!" Elaine said. "But you're quite right. He is very nice."

"It's supposed to be frightfully good luck to be given a gift by one," Lydia continued as they wandered on through the market. "They say it can protect you at sea." Lydia then abruptly changed the subject. "I'm hungry. Do you know anywhere we can eat?"

"Of course. And drink! It's this way." Elaine quickly took the lead heading along a small lane away from the bustling market into the older part of town. Going from memory, she took them down a series of alleys that twisted and turned through the tightly packed houses. Eventually they came to one that was particularly narrow. Lydia looked about her in sudden alarm. This was most certainly not the sort of alley Miss Drake would approve of!

"Here we are," Elaine said cheerfully stopping by a plain door in a wall. "This is where I come with Father sometimes. Don't be put off by the outside, that's just to keep people away!" She opened the door and ushered Lydia inside. They found themselves in a narrow hallway lit by a single lantern that had formerly belonged to a warship. At the end was another low door from beyond which came the sound of voices. This door took Lydia into her first tavern. As an experience it couldn't have been more of a shock given that it was a unique establishment.

A former First Mate, when he retired from the sea, had been determined to create a tavern unlike any other and had opened "The Mermaid's Rest". He had proceeded to recreate the interior of a ship's main cabin, albeit on a larger scale, in as much detail as was possible. The windows at the far end of the room had been rebuilt into a sweeping curve to mimic the stern of a large ship. Every fixture and fitting in the room had been "obtained" from various ships and dockyards to give an air of authenticity to the experience. His second stroke of genius had been to locate the tavern in such a remote part of town that the only people who drank there were friends and local sailors, none of whom ever gave him any trouble.

"Miss Elaine! What a pleasure. Not with your father today?" The owner's face was open and welcoming. He was a man of at least sixty years of age with a face lined by the sun and the wind. He had clear blue eyes and his grey hair was tied back in the traditional plaited ponytail.

"Hello Edward! No, I sailed down the coast with my cousin Lydia today," Elaine said, settling herself on a stool at one end of the curved bar (another naval innovation).

"And had a spot of bother with your mainsail?" the old sailor enquired with a twinkle in his eyes. "Very nice to make your acquaintance Miss Lydia." Lydia smiled politely as she settled down next to Elaine.

"News travels fast!" grumped Elaine. "Perhaps rather than criticising my boat handling you might offer us some food and something to drink?"

"Of course. It's a bit late, but we have some soup left, perhaps with bread roll and some biscuit for afters?"

"Sounds great!" The man turned and bustled out to a small kitchen behind the bar.

"This is, um, different," Lydia remarked.

"It's the best tavern on the island," Elaine told her. "Best thing of all, it's quite safe. Some of the taverns are very rough, you know. Edward's known me since I was about four, I think. He and Father are old friends. They sailed together before he married my mother and settled down at TolSor. If we're lucky, Old Joe, that's the grey bearded chap in the corner there, will give us a few of his songs before we go. The man next to him is his son, Young Joe; he's a fantastic fiddle player. He lost his left leg aboard HMS Thunder. A cannon crushed him when it broke free in a storm."

At this point Edward returned with their food. The two girls were very hungry and they quickly tucked in.

"This is delicious!" Lydia said immediately. "What is it?"

"Albatross meat," Edward said. "Fine eating on those birds; very little fat you see Miss Lydia."

"It's very nice, thank you," Lydia replied not noticing the stifled guffaws of those in earshot.

"And what would you like to drink Miss Elaine? Don't bother asking for rum, your mother would have my hide!"

"Sweet mead please, Edward," Elaine answered.

"I'd like ale please!" Quite why Lydia said that was anyone's guess, it just sort of came out. No one seemed to think anything of it though. Shortly afterwards Elaine had a slim glass of mead in front of her and Lydia had a frothing pint of ale.

Surprisingly, the taste was quite pleasant and the sensation in her stomach a moment later was not all that bad either. Lydia munched on a biscuit and sipped on her ale. She felt content and amazingly free of the constraints of Wescliffe and school.

The two Joes did indeed sing a few sea shanties with which Elaine and the other patrons joined in. Lydia joined in any choruses and tapped her feet more or less in time depending how fast the tune was. It was in the midst of one of these songs that two stooped figures entered the bar through the low door. At first neither girl noticed them but as they approached the bar the music fell abruptly silent. A hush descended on the room. These were not "regulars".

One of the strangers was wearing the distinct uniform of a marine. The other was in a deep blue greatcoat with the gold markings of a junior naval officer.

"Gentlemen, welcome to the Mermaid. What would you like?" Edward's eyes were wary but his voice warm and friendly.

"Nothing, thank you. We're on the King's business here." The junior officer spoke sharply and without a trace of friendliness. "We are looking for someone. I wonder if your patrons have seen him?"

"Pray name him and I'll tell you." Edward's bearing had relaxed. He knew his drinkers well enough to know that they'd not be in this sort of trouble – at least, if they were he'd have known.

"Tristan D'Shan," the officer replied shortly. "Have you seen or heard of him? Any information at all would be most welcome. There's a high price on his head. I warn you; failure to give information will result in most severe punishment."

"Well now," Edward appeared to be thinking; his eyes looking past Lydia (who had gone very still indeed) as though she weren't there. "That would be the governor's eldest, I believe? Went away must have been two, three years ago now? I don't think he's been seen on the island since, to my knowledge at any rate. He wouldn't be all that welcome if he had to tell you the truth. No. I've not seen or heard of him. I'd tell you quick enough if I had, Lieutenant. No love lost for that family here!" The Lieutenant nodded, accepting Edward's statement without much reaction. He and his companion turned, evidently intending to question the rest of the room. Lydia felt panic rising within her.

"Damn you for a fool!" The bellow came from over by the window. Young Joe had seemingly knocked a five-pint pitcher of ale over the two sailors at the table next to his. The youngest of these, who seemed to have already got through a few pints judging by the unsteady way he grabbed the table, rose to his feet with fists clenched. With an alarmed shout Edward darted out from behind the bar and placed himself between the two men. Only Elaine caught the quick wink and a smile once the two visitors' attention had been diverted.

"No trouble here, gentlemen," he warned.

"Fool yourself!" Young Joe snarled, provoking a drunken lunge in his direction that almost connected with Edward. The marine stepped forward to assist and at this point Lydia's paralysis was broken by Elaine's hand pulling her towards the door. A moment later they were outside heading up the alley.

"Slow down a bit Elaine!" Lydia complained. She had been comfortable enough in the bar but this sudden movement was throwing up some unexpected difficulties. For one thing, the ground seemed very unsteady.

"Best keep moving until we're away," Elaine insisted continuing through the maze of narrow passages at a brisk pace. A moment later she heard a thump from behind her. Turning, she saw that Lydia had tripped and gone flying into a filthy drainage gully. "Oh, are you alright?" Elaine ran back to her. Lydia was giggling helplessly, tears streaming down her face. "Lydia?"

"What?" Lydia was suddenly serious again.

"Are you alright?"

"My dress!" It was too much. With a splutter Lydia was off Into another fit of the giggles. She tried to stand up but the difficulty with that made her laugh even more. "Go on," she gasped. "I think I'll stay right here!"

"Oh, Lydia! You mean you've never had ale before? Why didn't you say? Look at the state of you! We've got to get back to the boat yet. *Do* come on!"

In the end Elaine had to drag Lydia to her feet and support her most of the way back to where the sailor was waiting for them. Somehow Elaine got her cousin down the steps but from there she fell, giggling, into the bottom of the boat. "We'd like to go back now," Elaine said with as much dignity as possible. The sailor's face betrayed none of his thoughts.

"Very well, Miss." They rowed out to SKYLARK in silence – apart from the singing from the bottom of the boat. Getting Lydia aboard ship ended up being a two-person effort that cost Elaine an extra penny out of gratitude for the sailor. Even his experience and strength couldn't prevent Lydia slipping and dunking herself in the harbour. He did fish her out quite expertly though. They got her aboard on the second attempt. Elaine paid the fee and the tip – then turned her attention to Lydia.

The sudden immersion in very cold water had cured the giggles but she was now shivering. There were no dry clothes to change into so Elaine simply had to wrap her in some waterproof covers and hope for the best. They were close to missing their tide. She quickly readied the sails before returning to the stern.

"Lydia, you need to take the tiller, just while I get the sails up and slip the mooring. Listen out and try to do what I say, alright?" Lydia nodded, her teeth rattling like castanets. "That's my girl!" Elaine grinned. With the exception of the next few moments, Lydia's situation was really quite amusing. She would never have thought she'd see the day; Lydia tipsy! Elaine chuckled to herself as she began to haul on the jib sheet.

In the event they slipped their mooring without incident. SKYLARK turned, caught the wind and turned further before Lydia managed to steady her on a course taking them out into the centre of the bay. The sun still shone brightly while the wind had strengthened a bit, awakening a slight increase in the swell. As Elaine began to hoist the mainsail she was unaware of the effect this new factor was having on the helmswoman.

Lydia was not feeling well. The motion of the boat was not helping and the bright light reflecting off the water hurt her eyes. Concentrating on not being sick, she was not particularly watching where she was going.

A large percentage of HMS Hunter's crew were ashore looking for Tristan D'Shan but not all. Two of the main-deck gun crews had borrowed a pair of longboats and were having a race across the harbour to settle a bet. In times gone by, such rivalry would have been resolved through gunnery practice but the navy was economising these days. The guns were seldom fired even in practice. A boat race had seemed like a good idea. To ensure fair play two midshipmen, whose status as "gentlemen" prevented any cheating, captained each longboat.

The "Starboard" crew were presently winning by three boat lengths. The Cox, whose job it was to steer the boat, had half an eye on the marker buoy for the halfway point and the other half behind on the opposition. By simple mathematics that didn't leave enough attention to spot a racing yacht on a converging course gathering speed fast.

The crew were first to spot the danger. The slower-witted ones shouted a warning. The intelligent ones abandoned their oars – and the boat – as quickly as possible. Puzzled by the sudden reduction in speed, both Cox and midshipman turned just in time to see SKYLARK sweeping down on their little craft. There was no time to react before the forefoot struck the longboat just aft of the bows and crashed onwards; cutting the boat in half as though under a vengeful guillotine. A moment later they were all swimming.

Elaine felt the unmistakable shudder of the impact as she was making her way aft to relieve Lydia. Just as she got to the cockpit Lydia abandoned the tiller to be terribly ill over the side of the boat. Elaine seized the tiller and looked sharply astern. A few bits of longboat and perhaps ten heads bobbed in their wake.

"Oh hell!" she exclaimed, preparing to put SKYLARK about to render assistance. A sharp crack from the second longboat changed her mind.

Midshipman Browne, a youth of thirteen years of age, had scarcely spotted the danger to his rival before they were sunk by the large yacht. His outrage at this terrible bit of seamanship turned to something else when he spotted the D'Shan flag at the stern. Knowing that Tristan D'Shan was both dangerous and wanted by the King, he rapidly came to the conclusion that the act must have been deliberate. The head in the stern was barely visible. Browne presumed the fugitive at the tiller was trying to hide from him. He swiftly pulled out his pistol and fired off a shot.

"Bloody hellfire!" The pistol ball embedded just a few inches from Elaine's head. On instinct, she altered course a little earlier than intended to bring SKYLARK onto its best point of sailing. Using every trick she knew, Elaine coached the maximum speed out of the boat that she could; taking them rapidly out of range to sea.

"What was that?" Lydia asked weakly. She was a sort of green colour but beginning to feel better.

"Oh, nothing!" Elaine replied with some irony. "We just sank a Royal Navy ship and got shot at!" Lydia pulled herself up and looked aft. The second longboat was conducting rescue operations for the crew of its erstwhile competitor.

"Oh, my! Did I do that?"

"'Fraid so!" Elaine confirmed.

"Father's going to kill me," Lydia predicted miserably feeling suddenly very sober.

"*Us*, Lydia. He's going to kill *us*. Of course, they might not mention it. After all, they did shoot at us and I'd guess that wouldn't go down too well with your father. Probably, though, we're for it!"

They sailed on in silence watching the light fade until, with an impressive display of skill, Elaine brought SKYLARK into Wescliffe Cov. The anchor was lowered and the ship secured for the night. By that time the girls had just enough energy to climb the steep path to the house. They staggered off to bed leaving their tea uneaten.

Lydia awoke the next morning feeling decidedly unwell. Not only did she ache all over but she had a pounding headache. This was not improved when the housekeeper discovered her ruined clothes. She decided to spend the day in bed. This was partly to avoid awkward questions from her cousin about the incident yesterday at the tavern. The shock of hearing Tristan's name again, after three years in which to forget it, had yet to wear off. Lydia needed time to think about her own feelings before speaking to Elaine on the subject.

Elaine had no such worries, being more used to taverns than Lydia. After a quick breakfast, she made her way down to the cov and SKYLARK. Rowing around the boat, she was horrified at the damage the collision had caused. The varnish around the bows and along the port side waterline was horribly scratched. Coupled with the dirty sail and the small matter of the pistol ball embedded in the woodwork, there was a lot to be done. The next two hours were filled with the business of getting SKYLARK out of the water and back into the boathouse. Two stable hands were recruited to operate the windlass with her. By the evening, "her" boat was back in the launching position and work was underway on the repairs.

Elaine saw very little of her cousin for the next three days. The incident with the longboat thankfully never came to light but the ruined dress was enough to secure three days of torture under her mother's supervision. Lydia was obliged to spend her days with Mrs D'Shan in the day room receiving guests, listening in silence to their chatter and making tapestry.

Elaine, meanwhile, worked contentedly on SKYLARK. The boathouse was well equipped with tools. Those it lacked were borrowed from various members of the household with little more effort than a charming smile. The only slight cloud, upon these otherwise carefree but hard-working days, was an occasional sense of unease - as though she was being watched. It was like a chill wind blowing through the boathouse even when all the doors were shut.

This unease was fleeting. For most of the time Elaine was thoroughly absorbed in her work. She felt an obligation - a duty almost - towards the boat. She worked hard and carefully to repair and touch up the damage.

By the time Lydia gave her the good news that the holiday could begin again there was no evidence, except to the most professional of eyes, that SKYLARK had ever put to sea. Having worked so hard even Elaine's appetite for sailing could not motivate her to re-launch the boat. They opted to go riding instead. Days slipped by without further incident. The girls allowed themselves if not to forget the trip to Perth Cathe, to at least place it at the back of their minds.

Chapter Four - Unwelcome Guests

Three days later, on returning to Wescliffe after a day out, the girls found the house bustling with activity. Lydia's mother greeted them at the door with a scowl.

"Girls! Look at the state of you! You are to be changed and presentable for dinner tonight. We have an important guest. Now, run along." She turned to the Housekeeper. "Miss Haldon, hot water to the girls' rooms at once and for heaven's sake try to find something nice for Elaine to wear!"

"Something nice" turned out to be a dress that didn't fit Lydia with some hasty alteration to the hem. The fact that the dress had been made for Lydia, rather than for her, caused Elaine to become acquainted for the first time with that most unpleasant item of clothing; the corset.

"Heavens, Lydia! How do you put up with these things?" she complained walking stiffly into Lydia's room. "I'm not even sure I can sit down wearing this!"

"They are pretty awful," Lydia agreed. She was looking her best but Elaine was beginning to realise the sacrifice to personal comfort that such a look entailed. "Just remember not to eat much. They can become unbearable if you do. Small mouthfuls and leave at least half on your plate. Polite society does not place much value on a healthy appetite!"

"Great!" Elaine grumped. "What's the occasion then?"

"Some Ladyship visiting Father, evidently." Lydia shrugged impatiently. "Awful timing as usual! I was looking forward to a quiet evening by the fire. Now we'll probably have to be seen-and-not-heard all evening." She shuddered. "I hope Mother doesn't make us sing."

In the room below Lydia's, Thomas D'Shan was having an uncomfortable time. He was sat in his own visitor's chair watching Lady Denmir examine the Revenue Ledger behind his desk. Lady Denmir was still on the right side of thirty and, in a soft light, might be considered pretty. Beyond that there was little reason for Thomas to welcome her surprise visit. Of all the King's Revenue Inspectors, she had the worst reputation for spotting errors. However, it was not the errors that were worrying him. He decided to break the silence and test the waters.

"I trust all is in order, Lady Denmir?" he ventured. "As you can see, revenues are up on last year.

"Tax revenues are indeed, Mr D'Shan," she replied without looking up. There had been a very slight emphasis on the word "mister" which did not go unnoticed. "Import duties have not altered at all," she continued. "This is at odds with the other islands. Furthermore, seizures of un-revenued goods are well down on last year." Thomas decided that attack was the best form of defence.

"We do not tolerate smuggling here, Lady Denmir. The evidence indicates that organised smuggling has been stamped out!"

"I see." A pair of blue eyes now rose from the page to stare straight at him. "And disorganised smuggling is tolerated then?"

"Ah, ha!" The nervous laugh sounded false even to him. "Your Ladyship is pleased to jest, surely?"

"My husband tells me I lack a sense of humour, Mr D'Shan." That, Thomas realised, was the reason she was pretty but not beautiful. Beauty comes from within and Lady Denmir had the personality and emotion of an accountant. There was just no humanity in the woman. Thomas wondered irrelevantly what her husband thought about that but hastily dismissed the thought. "Small vessels can bring in goods quicker and easier than the old runners," she continued, her tone of voice unmistakably that of one giving a lecture to a slow-witted pupil. "This has been found to be the case on the island of Elledran and elsewhere. Your fellow Revenue Officers have been quick to respond to the change in tactics. You have not." This last sentence was brutal and to the point.

"My dear Lady!" Thomas was not accustomed to such a dressing down and his temper stirred at the insult. "I assure you, we have been very active and...."

"And yet you have seized no goods, nor have any criminals been apprehended!" Lady Denmir fixed him with a withering stare. "Monies are paid out but to no gain. This I find disturbing." Thomas had no choice but to defend himself although he could spot a losing battle as well as the next man.

"Your Ladyship, if Lieutenant Cartwright is to have men watch a beach all night, he and his men must be paid!" Lady Denmir made a disdainful gesture.

"If men are to spend a night watching a beach upon which nothing happens I see no reason why His Majesty should be expected to pay! I notice that certain sums are paid monthly to a Mr Groth. Perhaps if his information is unreliable it should be his purse that bears the cost?" Thomas felt an ice-cold panic in the pit of his stomach. This was getting serious.

"Revenue Officers have discretion, Ma'am, over payment to certain individuals. It would be... unwise to adopt the approach you suggest." Lady Denmir finally lost her temper at that point. She had been assessing the character of the man opposite her. She was not favourably impressed.

"Mr D'Shan, it is I who have discretion. Discretion and authority to decide who is and who is not worth the money they cost His Majesty! I have business on the islands of Nellad then Ror. In two months I shall return. Meantime, you will speak to Mr Groth. You will tell him that in the hold of my vessel are seven crates of un-revenued goods purchased by my crew at Perth Calran, Perth Cathe and Pathmeet. You will tell him that in one week I have arrested and hanged seven smugglers! You will get from him the information you need to give me real results in two months that will save your job. If he cannot, I suggest you dispose of his services!"

"Your Ladyship!" Thomas had sat up in his chair, transfixed and horrified by the bluntness of her words. "I shall attend to it."

"Very well, we shall let it rest there." Lady Denmir closed the ledger with a thump. It was a gesture, Thomas thought, which might well reflect his own career and future. Despite this he was a man who valued etiquette and good manners very highly. The harsh telling off did not change that.

"I trust we shall have the pleasure of your company for dinner tonight, your Ladyship? The nights are drawing in and the weather often worsens after sunset. We can offer you and your attendants a room for the night." Lady Denmir allowed herself to be surprised by the offer. She had not expected Thomas to be so gracious.

"Thank you, that is most generous. I would be honoured to accept your hospitality."

It was an awkward meal. Despite the best efforts of the adults to make cheerful small talk, Lydia could tell that something was wrong. Her father looked uncomfortable while her mother was clearly displeased about something. Elaine said very little during the meal. Despite being desperately hungry she managed not to eat all her food. As Lydia had predicted, her already tight corset became positively painful after the smallest of meals.

Things looked like they were going to get worse before they got better. The adults adjourned to the day room after the meal. The girls were naturally expected to go too. They sat quietly, smiling politely when the conversation was about them. The adults never addressed them directly but had a habit of speaking about them as though they weren't there.

The whole experience was new for Elaine who, despite Lydia's frequent complaints, rather believed that her cousin had a very privileged and comfortable life. This application of Miss Drake's lessons in "deportment and etiquette" made her realise how desperately boring such an existence must be for someone of Lydia's intelligence and energy.

"And Lydia's very musical," Mrs. D'Shan continued. She's going to ask me to sing, Lydia realised painfully. Just when I thought it couldn't get worse! "Do play us something, dear," Mrs D'Shan said, gesturing to the piano. As an option, it wasn't much better than a song since Lydia had been neglecting her practice recently.

"Does your niece play?" Lady Denmir enquired. "A duet, perhaps?"

"Oh, Elaine does not play pianoforte as far as I am aware. Her parents are not that wealthy, you know. Her father is responsible for the beacon tower on the Sor coast."

"I see." The tone of those two words, coupled with the rather crushing nature of the preceding remarks stung Elaine's pride.

"I play flute," she said helpfully. By speaking at all she had broken etiquette and her aunt frowned.

"Perhaps you could play something with Miss Lydia?" Lady Denmir enquired.

"I'll get my flute," Elaine said, standing so quickly that her head swam briefly from the tight corset. "Do please excuse me!" This lady-like comment was followed by some most unlady-like language as she went upstairs to collect the Sprite's flute from her room. She was careful not to return too quickly. She was sure her aunt would not be able to resist another put-down if she was seen to rush.

"What can you play?" Lydia whispered as they readied themselves at the piano. "I've never heard you play that thing! You only got it the other day!"

"Don't worry," Elaine reassured her quietly. "Just play something simple and repeat it a few times. I'll come in the second time through."

"I'll play Lords and Ladies," Lydia announced. It was a short simple tune that she had learned that term. She played it through and sure enough, on the first repeat, Elaine's flute joined the piano with an accompaniment which lifted the simple tune into something altogether more complicated and beautiful.

The flute's tone was pure, without a trace of shrillness. The sound of it filled the room, first blending with and then soaring above the piano's simple melody. Elaine's fingers seemed to instinctively move whilst the tone and volume rose and fell in an intricate yet haunting pattern. The girls played for about two minutes before finishing with a final note which gently faded leaving the audience in stunned silence.

At Math Calran, the Governor was experiencing another interrupted evening caused by an unexpected guest. As he entered the study, a robed figure rose from his seat and turned to greet him.

"Governor, thank you for seeing me."

"A pleasure Master Berant, though an unexpected one." Galvin D'Shan gazed sharply at his guest's face as he shook his hand. "How may I be of service?" Daren Berant allowed the Governor to sit before answering him.

"I understand there is a difficulty. You had a visit..."

"Nothing to worry about," the governor cut him short. "I have matters in hand."

"I very much doubt that, my Lord. You cannot meet this threat with militiamen, nor yet Marines, however well trained they may be. You know this."

"I know my Island, Master Berant, just as I know my son. He is wilful - not pleasant certainly - and he is wont to bluster. If he sees Fain-Arn is not a comfortable place for him he will move on. I have just to stir up enough activity and he will find this place is not to his liking."

"I think you underestimate the danger." Daren spoke gently. "He is far more powerful than when he left the island. Tristan is a real danger to those you send to find him. This situation requires a different approach."

"Your jurisdiction is confined to within the reach of the tide if memory serves, Master Berant." The Governor's voice took on a shrewish tone. "I fail to see why this matter concerns the Guild of Navigators. Do not presume to over-reach yourself."

"I am merely here as escort to the Mageseekers." Daren waved his hand dismissively. "I have no direct interest in the matter." He waited for the Governor to relax in his chair. "Except for this. Tristan represents a destructive and evil force which will not remain confined to this island, nor even the Kingdom. The Kerun Dur will not allow one of his kind to remain unchecked and unchallenged. It is for the Kerun Dur that I must ensure the situation is resolved."

"I am dealing with the matter. I do not expect interference." Galvin D'Shan rose to his feet. After a brief pause, Daren joined him. His blue eyes met those of the Governor.

"I very much hope it won't be necessary, my Lord, for everyone's sake. I shall take my leave." With a polite nod of the head Daren left the room. The Governor of Fain-Arn sank wearily back into his chair.

The following day brought a return of the wet miserable weather that had greeted the girls on their return to Wescliffe. A fire was lit in the old nursery. The girls spent the day trying – and mostly failing – to relieve the boredom. For much of the time Elaine stared out of the window watching drops running down the pane. The truth was she was uneasy. There was no reason for it, unless she was mistaking the symptoms of simple homesickness, but for the entire day she was jumpy and on edge. The chill she had experienced in the boathouse returned. This time she found it impossible to shake off. Lydia interpreted the signs as something else and gave her friend the space she needed.

The low cloud cover meant that dusk fell earlier than usual. Although Wescliffe was not a poor house, the girls were encouraged to use their own rooms after dark to save on candles (oil was only used for important guests and formal occasions). After tea, the wind began to rise steadily, echoing in the chimney and casting spray noisily against Lydia's window. The pair were dressed for bed but had no intention of retiring just yet. Elaine complained at least once per day about how unfair it was that the only comfortable clothes she could wear (her normal "working" clothes were not suitable for Wescliffe) were for sleeping in.

In an effort to lift Elaine's spirits, Lydia had suggested a game of chess to pass the evening. This was a noble suggestion on her part. Lydia possessed all the tactical brilliance of the Wheldorian Admiral who had once led a squadron of eight line-of-battle ships onto the treacherous chain of rocks to Fain-Arn's Est.

Noble though Lydia's intentions were, however, Elaine's mind was not on the game. Despite some brilliantly stupid moves, Lydia found herself winning. Not wanting to make Elaine feel worse, Lydia had been searching for a way out that might allow her cousin to lose with some dignity. That required a level of forward planning that she was not accustomed to. Lydia decided to stall and allow Elaine time to think.

"I'm thirsty," she said. "I'll only be a minute, Elaine. I'm going to nip down to the kitchen. I might be able to steal something nice if Cook's in a good mood. You stay here in the warm!" On the way out, Lydia grabbed a night robe from the hook behind the door. Wescliffe was a very draughty house, particularly on nights such as this.

The hall was in almost total darkness when she got to the bottom of the stairs. Just a little light spilled out under the door from the waiting room to her father's office. Lydia was barefoot and so moved silently across the polished boards towards the dining room. She had scarcely taken a few steps when a shadow moved suddenly from the deeper darkness under the stairs.

"Miss D'Shan!"

"What?" The word came out almost as a short scream. In the bedroom upstairs, Elaine stirred. The sense of uneasiness returned with a sudden desperate urgency.

"Ah! Do not be alarmed. I startled you. I do apologise." The voice was smooth and polite. The figure of a man Lydia had seen a few times before emerged further into the half-light. As he spoke, he bowed apologetically in a perfect display of good manners. Lydia took a deep breath to regain her shaken composure but remained slightly on guard.

"You are forgiven," she assured him, wanting to get the meeting over as swiftly as possible. Any thought of the kitchen had gone but the figure was between her and the stairs. "You are?" The question hung in the air.

"Here to see your father, my dear," the man replied smoothly. "How you have grown! There is much of your mother about you. You have become quite a young lady I see." The tone was very familiar, like that of an uncle or close family friend. As he spoke he took another step towards her. On pure instinct, Lydia took another step back. "But schooling helps I daresay and Miss Drake is an excellent teacher. You had a pleasant trip to Perth Calran I gather! I trust you got home without further incident?"

"Indeed," Lydia replied, desperately trying to think of a way to escape. "My father is expecting you?" This was intended as a prompt to end the conversation but it failed.

"Keeping me waiting as ever!" the man replied with a dry laugh. "Thus am I reminded of my humble position. Your father likes to make a point, Lydia." This use of her first name brought a slight flush of colour to Lydia's cheeks. It was utterly impolite of the man since she hardly knew him. He had taken another step towards her which she mirrored with a step back of her own. The cold panelling of the wall was against Lydia's back now and there was nowhere to go. "Such games can be dangerous," the man continued. "They have two players you see. Your father should remember that! I can make a point too."

The man's bearing changed subtly. He was very close to her now. He seemed to bring a shadow of darkness with him and Lydia began to feel real fear. "Everyone has their weakness," he spoke softly and deliberately. "For some it is money. For your father it is you." His hand reached out to touch Lydia on the cheek. She was so paralysed by the sudden cold terror this man's presence seemed to cause that she remained utterly still. Elaine's clear voice shattered the moment.

"Lydia! There you are!" In an instant, the man's hand was withdrawn. His shoulders relaxed and he turned to Elaine with a genial smile on his face.

"And this must be Miss Elaine!" The tactic was not destined to succeed. Elaine cut him short, her voice ice cold.

"I don't think I know you!" The tone was an almost perfect imitation of Mary Newton at her most snobbish.

"Indeed not! How impertinent of me." The man seemed to have trouble meeting Elaine's steady stare and so he turned instead to Lydia. "Well, Lydia, I enjoyed our chat but I think I should go and interrupt your father's important work. Ladies!" He bowed and swept through the door of the waiting room, closing it behind him.

"Creep!" Elaine's voice remained angry and scornful. "Who is he to use our first names? He lacks manners!" Elaine noticed that her friend was very pale and trembling. "Are you alright?"

"Fine," Lydia replied a little uncertainly. Then pulling herself together, "No, really! That man... I find him a bit scary.

"Your father will take care of him." Elaine's impression of the man was very different to Lydia's. To Elaine he appeared rude and weak. His inability to face her down was a sign of a weak character in her opinion. In this she was only partly correct. Lydia's impression had been rather more alarming. The manner in which he had transformed from being polite, to menacing, to polite had quite unsettled her.

"He's often around..." Lydia tried to put into words the fears which suddenly beset her. "I think he must watch me. He seems to know far more about what I do than Father or Mother; our trip the other day, for instance.

"You should speak to your father, Lydia, really you should!" Elaine spoke seriously, shocked at the sudden transformation that had come over her cousin. "He'd not last five minutes! I know he's distant but your father cares about you and he's an influential man. I'm quite sure he'd make short work of putting that over-familiar oaf in his place!"

"I may mention it... when I get a chance." That required some more thought. The man had seemed confident that in threatening her, he was threatening her father too. Lydia decided not to mention that to Elaine for now. She just wanted to return to the safety of her room. "Let's go back upstairs. You're losing a chess game, remember?"

"Losing? I think not!" Elaine huffed. "Just... forming a plan, that's all."

"You lose any more pieces to my bishop and it'll be the first time in history a king's won all by itself!" Lydia retorted.

"Hey! It's a silly rule that they can go diagonally!" Elaine protested. "Anyway, maybe that's the clever part of the plan!" The two headed back upstairs bickering amiably.

In Thomas D'Shan's office an altogether different game was being played out. There was nothing amiable about it. Groth simply entered without knocking irritating Mr D'Shan who, as Groth had correctly guessed, was keeping him waiting to make a point. Groth compounded the insult by taking a seat unasked.

"Sorry to intrude, your Lordship, but time is pressing. You wanted to see me?" The tone, along with the fictitious title, was insolent.

"Your dry sense of humour remains I see, Groth!" D'Shan replied calmly. "Yes, I sent for you. We have a problem."

"We?" Groth raised an eyebrow theatrically and leaned back in the chair.

"You!" D'Shan clarified shortly. "Lady Denmir does not think you are providing value for money."

"And you?" Groth almost yawned but thought that might be overdoing it. Thomas D'Shan was overly inclined to panic. Groth never panicked. He rarely troubled himself with being "concerned". He was not that sort of person.

"I have little to say in the matter it seems," D'Shan replied bitterly. "She wants results and fast. The next shipment must be intercepted. Regrettable, but necessary." Groth's relaxed manner did not alter a bit, but he became very still.

"That will cause problems, Sir. It will anger our friends and damage the operation." His voice was quiet and reasonable. D'Shan, unfortunately, was not feeling very reasonable at this moment in time.

"Damn it!" he snapped. "We won't *have* an operation if that woman gets her way."

"Beg pardon, Sir," Groth interrupted smoothly, "but *you* won't have an operation. I would of necessity deal with your replacement. They will, in time, come to see the way things work here." Thomas kept his temper under control with some considerable effort. *Groth is getting a bit too confident*, he thought. *Perhaps he might need reminding of his place.*

"Groth! Do not take that tone with me! I am in charge here. The next shipment will be stopped. It will damage us temporarily but only temporarily. This will pass. You do not need the complication of a new and scrupulous Revenue Officer!" Which was a fair point, Thomas thought. Unfortunately, Groth saw it differently.

"You may weather temporary inconveniences better than I!" he said calmly. "You have your status and money. I on the other hand..."

"You are paid well enough!" Thomas cut him short. "Tighten your belt and keep out of games where the stakes are beyond your purse!" That got a reaction, Thomas saw. The man was rattled. *Good. Some salt for the wound.* "Yes!" he continued, "I, too, have sources Groth! Your vice is well known. Give the cards a rest."

In fact, Thomas had learned of Groth's gambling troubles by chance, rather than by design, but there was no way Groth would know that he judged. Groth's voice became quieter still but took on a hint of the edge it had contained earlier in the hallway.

"It would seem fairer, Sir, since your ineptitude led us to this that you reimburse me for the inconvenience yourself." D'Shan came to his feet as though lifted by an explosive charge.

"You insolent whelp!" he exploded. "How dare you! Get out!" The last two words rattled the windows and carried clearly through the ceiling to the room above where Lydia and Elaine paused their game and shared a knowing look.

"I told you! He's for it now," Elaine said.

In the study Groth, too, was on his feet. Some of his composure had fallen away. His eyes were cold and he met Thomas's angry stare with contempt.

"I can break you, D'Shan. I will survive because I always do! You have far too much to lose. Your status, your home," he paused for emphasis, "your family."

"Do not threaten me, Groth! I warn you. Do not cross me!" Thomas was almost shaking with rage and yet his voice was controlled. Groth laughed in his face.

"You are a weak man, Thomas. I spoke to Lydia just now. A fine girl and grown so fast. Can you watch her every hour? I think not! Are you near her when she rides out across the downs alone? I think not! Can you save her when her boat sinks suddenly in the bay? You know not!" This lecture was delivered in a strong tone of voice. The implied threat was not lost on the man before him. Suddenly, Groth's whole bearing changed again. "I do not threaten you, Thomas, but warn you as a friend. My contacts are less understanding than I. Arrange my money and I'll get you your shipment. What real alternative do you have? Let us not fall out now."

Thomas stood motionless, his mind racing through his options. Groth watched the realisation dawn. The understanding that he was outmanoeuvred, that he was in too deep. That in dealing with Groth he placed his own survival in Groth's hands. A bitter realisation for a proud man but Groth felt no pity. He watched with sadistic pleasure as Thomas's shoulders sagged in defeat.

"Very well, Groth." D'Shan sat heavily in his chair.

"Excellent!" Groth's voice was clipped, business-like and polite once more. "I am sure this unpleasantness will pass. I trust you and yours will remain in the best of health until our next meeting." But D'Shan was not so easily cowed and his temper flared one last time.

"You have your deal, Groth! Dispense with the pleasantries and get from my sight!"

"As you wish, Sir." Groth bowed and departed the room.

The battle had been fought and both knew who was the victor. Groth knew he had pushed D'Shan very hard. Already his mind was looking ahead. A shipment would not make it to the buyers. Instead, the smugglers who hitherto had operated under the quiet arrangement between Groth and the man responsible for catching them would be arrested. *Perhaps there is an opportunity here to strengthen my hand*, Groth thought. Yes! There was a way to send a strong message about who was really in charge here. In the wild darkness of the night Groth grinned. What an opportunity this was! By selecting those who were caught he could eliminate several of the stronger characters in the organisation and emerge as the leader. And there was one person whose life he could blight into the bargain. *Oh yes, I'll see tears in those eyes before I'm through.*

Chapter Five - The Raid

Lydia did not sleep well that night. The wind buffeted about Wescliffe rattling her window and echoing in the chimney. The fire burned sulkily; its flames flickering low in the grate as the gusty blasts prevented the chimney from drawing properly. Shadows were cast about the room. On several occasions she awoke in terror thinking she saw a hand reaching for her out of the darkness. When she did sleep it was fretful; full of vague fears and the sense of someone wishing her ill.

Elaine noticed how pale Lydia looked at breakfast and that she was unusually quiet. She guessed the reason but was at a loss as to how to help. Elaine could hardly speak to Mr D'Shan herself; that would be better coming from Lydia. Instead Elaine showed her concern through kindness. She fetched things her cousin might need and offered to get her a hot drink from the kitchen. The gestures were appreciated but Lydia's spirits lifted slowly. It was mid-afternoon before she felt brave enough to face her father. For the second time, Lydia went through the waiting room and knocked at the study door.

At first there was no answer.

"Come!" a voice replied when she knocked again harder. On entering the study Lydia was horrified to see the state of her father. Normally a careful man in his appearance, today he was dishevelled. The clothes he wore were the same as the previous day. He had not shaved and his hair was a mess. Dark circles rimmed his eyes which were red. It was obvious that he had not left the study since the previous evening and he had got even less sleep overnight than her.

"Father! Is everything all right?" Lydia could not keep the concern from her voice but the man before her seemed not to hear. He was staring into the fireplace, which contained only ash since it had long since gone out. "Father?" Lydia repeated. Mr D'Shan stirred.

"Hmm? Ah, what is it dear?"

"I... wanted to speak to you. Are you busy?"

"Not especially my love," he replied. Lydia could only remember being "dear" once and never "my love". Generally, she was just "Child". It was almost as if he thought he was talking to someone else.

"It's about that man, the one who was here last night..." Thomas D'Shan leaped from his chair in agitation. He came over to her and gripped her arms tightly, staring into her face.

"Stay away from that man!" There was a wild urgent intensity about the stare and the voice. "Listen to me, Lydia! That man is poison! Stay away. Tell me if he comes near you again. You are not to leave the house for the rest of the holiday. You only have a short time left." His eyes lost their focus as he seemed to be thinking ahead. "Yes, I can have Smith escort you back to school. You should be safe there. When does school start?"

"Over a week and a half's time," Lydia replied shakily. Her father's grip was painful.

"You will stay in the house. That is understood?" Lydia nodded. "And you will forget about that man. He will not trouble you again. Not after tonight. Things will be right soon." He released his grip and looked suddenly much older and more vulnerable. "I'm sorry, Child, but things will be right. I just need time. Time..." He turned from her and slumped into the chair again.

"As you wish, Father." Lydia wanted to reach out to him. It seemed to her that he needed it. Their relationship was not close enough to permit that, however, so Lydia simply left him there alone. She returned upstairs to let Elaine know that things had not gone quite to plan.

"What?" Elaine was outraged. A week and a half of holiday remained. "Why, Lydia? Who is that creep anyway?" Lydia shook her head, equally frustrated.

"I don't know. He works for Father. I occasionally see him around. I think he's some kind of informant."

"A spy? That'd be about right! He's shifty enough! One of those characters who profit by others' misfortune." Elaine paced about the room, which she now regarded as a comfortable cage. "He threatens you and has a row with your father last night... but...." Her voice trailed off.

"It doesn't make sense," Lydia observed with a frustrated frown.

"No!" Elaine stopped pacing. "It doesn't, Lydia! Your father is much more powerful than him, surely? Can't he have people arrested if he wants to?"

"Smugglers, yes," Lydia shrugged. "I know Father is on good terms with Captain Skelder of the Militia. I would have thought he would just have to speak to him. Then there are always navy officers about. I'm sure they'd take care of him. I don't understand why Father's running scared."

The bell to the front door rang at that point. Before Lydia could object, Elaine dashed out of the room to look down the stairs. She returned a moment later.

"Speak of the devil," she grinned, returning a moment later. "Guess who just arrived? Captain Skelder himself. There's best part of a dozen men out front as well. I'm going to go and see what I can find out."

"Elaine, Father said..."

"Not to me he didn't!" Elaine was being cunning again. Lydia knew better than to argue.

"Just don't get caught," Lydia advised helpfully.

"Not me!" Elaine hurriedly pulled on her boots and grabbed a cloak. "I'll be back in a while!"

The yard was indeed crowded with Militia. Their breath steamed in the cold air as they lounged about in the easy manner of men with time on their hands. Their uniform coats were a dull burgundy, in contrast to the brighter red of the Marines or the royal green of the king's regular army. They were smart enough though; buttons and boots bright from hours of polishing, their faces confident and proud. Elaine scanned the group for a likely target and settled on a youngish chap with a couple of stripes on his arm.

"Excuse me?" she smiled brightly. "Could you help me?"

"Your servant, Miss," the young sergeant bowed politely.

"I was just wondering why you're all here," Elaine continued in her best empty-headed voice. "Is there some emergency?" The sergeant laughed.

"No, Miss, you're quite safe. We get called here from time to time. I expect the Revenue Officer wants us to arrest some smugglers tonight. If he gets information, we lie in wait for them, see?"

"Oh! I thought perhaps there was a criminal about."

"No. As far as I know the only criminals we're to worry about are the ones who bring in goods without paying their taxes." He smiled in a reassuring way.

"Is it dangerous, catching smugglers?" Elaine asked the question out of genuine interest. She generally heard about smuggling from the point of view of those who were sympathetic to the idea, rather than those tasked to enforce the law.

"Not particularly," the sergeant said complacently. "Hicks, bring over one of our toys from the cart!"

"Sarge!" A burly middle-aged man strolled over to a tarpaulin-covered cart and pulled a musket out from underneath the cover. He came across then handed it to the sergeant.

"You see, Miss, we are well able to defend ourselves!" The sergeant pointed the musket in show. "The King's Men are not to be messed with!"

"May I hold it?" Elaine's eyes lit up.

"Careful, it's heavy." He handed the musket over. Elaine took it and shifted her hands to get the balance right. She brought up the gun and sighted along it at a tuft of moss sticking out of the wall. CLICK. "Here!" the sergeant objected. "That might have been loaded!" Elaine gave him a look.

"Your man over there handed it to you muzzle downwards!" she reminded him. "How could it be loaded? Anyway, that was a misfire. I think your flint needs some attention."

"May I?" The sergeant took the musket, re-cocked the trigger and CLICK. No spark. "Humph!" he grunted. "You're right. So how does a young lady know so much about muskets?"

"We have a couple at home," Elaine told him. "I live at TolSor. Father told me that the King issued all the beacon towers with muskets when they were built. Some of the wreckers didn't like the towers much at first. Bad for business you see!" The sergeant nodded.

"Nasty times!" he agreed. "What sort of person wrecks a ship on purpose, eh? And us an island people. It's shameful. So your father taught you to fire these or just look after them?"

"Both," said Elaine at once. "Not much use looking after it if I can't fire it! Same thing firing it if I can't reload."

"Makes sense," the man agreed. "You reckon you can fix this?"

"Sure. You'd better check the others if they're the same as this!" Elaine had dropped the empty-headed girly act and was talking like Dan Sheldon's daughter once more. The sergeant chuckled.

"You'd be after my job, Miss?" Nonetheless he went over to the cart and, with Hicks, began to check the flints. After a few minutes, Elaine sighted the musket and this time the flint produced a spark. "That's a grand job," the sergeant acknowledged. "Can you fix this one as well?"

Lydia finally decided to go into Elaine's room after about twenty minutes and looked out of the window to see what her cousin was up to. She was utterly amazed to see Elaine working on a musket while chatting to one of the soldiers as though she had known him for years. She saw Elaine sight the gun in a professional manner before handing it to a soldier and picking up another.

It dawned on Lydia that just as there was much of her own life that was outside Elaine's experience, so there was much about her cousin's life that she did not know. Up until now Lydia had, for all her genuine friendship, felt some degree of superiority over her cousin. She knew that Elaine's family was very poor. Only through luck would Elaine ever be much better off than her parents.

Watching her now, Lydia wondered for the first time whether or not it might be Elaine who had the better deal. She was relaxed and chatting to a rather good looking young man in a manner which Lydia would certainly never be allowed to do. She was also doing something useful. Elaine's hands, though useless at tapestry, were amazingly skilled at practical tasks. The repairs to SKYLARK could not have been carried out better by the most expensive of Perth Cathe's shipwrights. Elaine could mend sails, tackle carpentry, make nets and, so it seemed, repair guns.

The thought occurred to Lydia that her cousin's horizons in life might be broader than her own whatever material hardship it might contain. To Elaine, the school and all its irritations were just an unpleasant interlude. For Lydia, the school's regime and lessons represented the rest of her life; a life of etiquette, marriage and unproductive use of her time. And babies of course. Her thoughts were interrupted by the slamming of the front door as Captain Skelder strode out into the yard.

The soldier with Elaine hastily hurried across to join his officer. They exchanged words briefly before Captain Skelder returned into the house. A flurry of orders followed which saw one soldier mount up and leave at the gallop. Shortly afterwards Elaine slipped away from the yard to re-join Lydia.

"You managed to tear yourself away then!" Lydia was shocked to hear the bitterness in her voice. "Sorry, Elaine, don't mind me. I'm just being a grump today."

"I didn't mean to be so long. I just sort of got chatting," Elaine said, dismissing the tension with a smile. "I've found out heaps. I think that the sergeant quite likes me. I guess he'd have been for it if those muskets hadn't been fixed."

"I couldn't help noticing how well you two were getting along," Lydia remarked mischievously. "Rather handsome isn't he? Married?"

"Lydia! Honestly!" Elaine blushed as intended. "He's a nice chap but not my type at all."

"Well, what is your type? You've never said. I'd have thought a handsome young army sergeant would be ideal. You seem to have a fair bit in common – guns for instance. What could be better?" Elaine picked up a pillow and buffeted her cousin with it.

"Leave it out would you? I'm not thinking of marrying just yet, alright? When I do, which won't be for a while, I'll start worrying about what type of man to find. 'Sides, he's engaged to someone over Pathmeet way. He told me."

"Oh, you did discuss it then? Ow!" Lydia received another energetic whack. "OK, I'll drop the subject.... for now. What did you find out then?" Elaine replaced the pillow and sat down on the bed.

"Loads. They're setting up an ambush to catch some smugglers. An informant – I'm guessing Mr Creep - has told your father there's going to be a landing tonight a few miles Sor of here. The militia are going to be waiting for them. Captain Skelder has sent one of his men to Perth Calran to get HMS Hunter to come down. She's moved up there from Perth Cathe I gather. Anyway, it all sounds very serious!"

"These raids are often quite big operations," Lydia said thoughtfully. "I've never heard of Father sending for the navy before though."

"I can tell you, those militiamen certainly mean business!" Elaine said. "And their muskets will work properly too," she added smugly. "I checked! You know..." she paused, looking out of the window to the sparkling surface of the Cathe in the distance. "If that creep set this thing up .... I wonder. Could it have anything to do with that row he had with your father last night?"

"How?" Lydia couldn't see a connection.

"I'm not sure," Elaine admitted. "I'm just wondering that's all. Something's going on between him and your father, Lydia, that's obvious. He thinks he can threaten you but the next minute he's helping your father catch smugglers. That doesn't seem right."

"I don't see what you mean," Lydia admitted, feeling rather dense.

"Look, one minute he's Mr Creep, the next he's the honest informant upholding the law and helping to catch criminals. I just don't think that adds up."

"Well, it does seem rather odd I suppose," Lydia agreed.

"I wonder…" Elaine had that look again. "They must be talking about that beach we passed on the way to Perth Cathe the other day. That's the only place where it would be safe to approach the shore in darkness. The sergeant said they'd be in the dunes all night, which makes sense because they can watch the beach from there. If we were on the ridge behind the dunes…. What do you think, Lydia?"

"About what?" Lydia had a nasty idea "what" but was living in hope.

"We could sneak out, take the horses and watch from the ridge. Perhaps we'll find out what's going on here. 'Sides, it'd be awfully exciting!"

"Elaine, you really are quite mad!" Lydia threw up her hands in frustration. "We'd never get away with it. Besides, it could be dangerous."

"Oh, rubbish!" Elaine was not easily put off. "The ridge is well out of range of any trouble and we'd have the horses to get away. The moon's out over the water, so we'd be in shadow whilst the beach would be all lit up. We could borrow the telescope from the library. Come on, Lydia, what do you say?"

"No!" said Lydia firmly. "Absolutely not!"

"I can't believe we're doing this!" Lydia was huddled miserably in the shelter of a bush whilst Elaine used the "borrowed" telescope to scan the beach. It was about eleven o'clock. The sky was relatively clear, which meant it was bitterly cold. The moon was waxing and would not reach full moon for about another week. It gave sufficient light for the night's planned activities however. A couple of meters away the tethered horses shifted about impatiently, wanting to get back to their warm stables.

"I think I can see Skelder's men over there," Elaine said eventually.

"Let's look then!" Lydia decided that since she was here she might as well make the most of things. She wriggled forwards to where Elaine was lying and took the telescope. She pointed it to where Elaine guided her. It took a while to get used to the light, but yes. "That's them alright!" she agreed. "There's another small group at the head of the beach, too. I think that sergeant of yours is with them." She handed the telescope back to Elaine who scanned the beach for a few more minutes.

"Looks like they're settling in," she said eventually. "I suppose now we wait and see."

"I stole some yeast buns from the larder if you're interested," Lydia said with her mouth full.

"Sounds good to me." The girls sat and munched for a while. "I like Fain-Arn at night," Elaine said on finishing her bun. "It's so still when the sky's clear like this."

"I don't think I've ever been out this late," Lydia replied. "Some of us think that night time is for sleeping, strangely enough!"

"Nights like this are about the only time we can get the boat out of CovTol," Elaine explained. "The currents by the rocks are very dangerous. Easy to get in, difficult to get out. Like a lobster pot, Father says. He sometimes takes me fishing at night. We drop our catch into Perth Cathe at first light and go for breakfast at The Mermaid. He doesn't go out in the boat so much these days."

"He's been quite ill, your father, hasn't he?" Lydia asked.

"Not so much recently but he was quite bad last year for a while," Elaine replied while looking through the telescope again. "He got a nasty fever. It kept him in bed for nearly three months and left him awfully weak. He still catches cold and the like very easily, especially on his chest. It affected his lungs, Mother told me."

"It must be hard for your mother," Lydia sympathised.

"Worse now she's got the baby but I'm older now. I can pretty much look after the tower." Elaine wriggled back from her vantage point. "No sign of anything. Of course, Father doesn't want me looking after the tower. That's why he sent me to school. He wants me to "better myself" whatever that means! I don't mind TolSor. I like being near the sea and I don't mind a bit of exercise. It beats washing clothes and changing baby."

"I suppose," Lydia wasn't really in a position to have an opinion on that particular subject. "I must admit, I quite like spending the odd day in the stables. It's nice to get out of the house. Some of the girls at school just ride their horses but I think it's important to be able to look after them as well. Of course, I can't as much as I'd like. Mother doesn't approve and John gets quite upset if I intrude into his domain!"

"He's very horse-proud is John," Elaine agreed. "No-one can look after the stables better than him."

"He used to work at Math Calran for the governor," Lydia said shifting her weight to get comfortable. "I think there was some sort of falling out so he came to work for us instead. He seems to be happy enough now."

"Well, he's left to do his job. That's pretty much all he wants I think." Elaine spread out her heavy sailing cloak on the ground and lay herself down, arms behind her head. Above her several stars were showing through the few wispy clouds. Elaine knew that the various clusters had names, but stargazing was not part of the curriculum at Harton and apart from Capradon, the Northern light, she didn't know what they were called. "Talking of the Governor," she continued, "when I was talking to those militiamen earlier they said they'd spent most of the week searching for his eldest son, Tristan. That was the chap those navy people were asking about in The Mermaid the other day. What's the story there?"

"We don't talk about him," Lydia replied bluntly.

"Sorry!" Elaine was surprised by the sharpness of the response. "It's just that, whatever he's done, they seem pretty serious about catching him. Dead or alive, the sergeant said."

"Doesn't surprise me," Lydia muttered. Then more clearly: "Look, Elaine, if I tell you, you have to keep it quiet. You can't tell any of your friends in Perth Cathe, or even your parents, alright?"

"Of course!" Elaine rolled onto her side to face Lydia.

"Tristan is a bit of a bad lot," Lydia explained quietly. "He's caused the family no end of trouble. The Governor's positively disowned him. I only met him a few times myself when I was very young. He was an obnoxious boy as I recall. Liked to kill things - he threw a dead rat at me once." Lydia shivered at the recollection of the childhood incident. It had taken her mother hours to calm her down afterwards. Tristan had just laughed. "The story is that he had a habit of getting a bit too friendly with the serving girls at Math Calran. It was so bad they couldn't get young staff at all for a while. Anyway, he ended up getting one girl pregnant – she wasn't the first but she was the daughter of a navy captain and they couldn't hush it up.

The girl's father demanded Tristan marry her and Tristan refused. They fought a duel and Tristan killed him. That's frightfully bad form, you understand. Duels hardly ever result in death. Anyway, this captain was a flag captain – serving with Admiral Heaton no less. There was a terrible scandal and Tristan was sent away. That's the official story. The real reason's much worse."

"Worse?" Elaine was aghast. What could possibly be a worse scandal than that for the island's aristocratic elite?

"I'm not supposed to know this but Mother and Father are so used to me being seen-and-not-heard that they sometimes think I'm deaf as well! Apparently, Tristan had The Gift. Hardly surprising, the Governor attended the Kerun Dur himself for a couple of years though I understand his gift is a minor one. Unfortunately, Tristan chose to apply The Gift to Dark Magic. He threatened to kill his own father, as well as cursing him. A weak curse but unpleasant. A mage from the King's court lifted it easily enough. Rumour has it that when Tristan was banished he intended to travel to Erath, to the Black Summit." Lydia shuddered. "That was about three years ago now. If he's back, and he's been there, he could be a powerful Void Mage."

"Well I never!" Elaine almost laughed, but refrained for fear of offending her cousin. "You lot certainly kept that quiet! Here was I thinking that the Sheldons were the disreputable branch of the D'Shan family! Don't worry, Lydia. I can't see a Void Mage popping up whilst the Mageseekers are on the island. There were four of them, don't forget. No matter how powerful this Tristan character thinks he is, he's not going to show up at the same time as those four. He'd have to be quite mad!"

"Perhaps," Lydia said ambiguously. From what she'd heard, Tristan D'Shan was the product of years of institutional arrogance surpassed only by royalty. She suspected that he wasn't the sort to give a damn about anyone much. What to Elaine was just a story about a black sheep in the family was somehow much more to Lydia. It hadn't been the dead rat that had so frightened her as a child but the look in Tristan's dark eyes when he did it. There was a side to him even then that had terrified her.

"Well, he's not our main worry right now." Elaine rolled over and reached for the telescope. "I'm going to take another look at the beach. You can have a snooze if you like. I'll wake you when I want to swap."

Midnight passed without incident. The wait was hard but the sight of the militia in hiding on the beach persuaded Elaine not to give up. They must be equally fed up, she reasoned, but were sitting tight. There was a light breeze from the Sor which ruffled the swell slightly out on the Cathe but otherwise the night was still. Owls called from their hunting grounds behind where the girls were hidden. Various nocturnal insects emerged and feasted on the unfortunate militia in the dunes who could do nothing more than utter strong oaths under their breath.

An hour and a half later, Elaine was seriously contemplating letting Lydia take a turn when she spotted movement away to her left. Four figures were moving steadily and cautiously towards the beach. Elaine swung the telescope sharply out to the horizon, searching the slate-grey hazy line between the night sky and the Cathe's surface. There! Low in the water under a single dark sail. A small craft which on any other night could not hope to survive in the Cathe so heavily loaded. Several heads bobbed in the craft and Elaine had no doubt that at least one telescope would be pointing her way. She wriggled carefully back from the ridge and gave the sleeping Lydia an unsympathetic prod.

"Rise and shine! The show's about to start."

"What time is it?" Lydia groaned, before remembering where she was and why. "Oh! What's going on?"

"The runners are out on the Cathe. Their friends will probably show a light in a minute or two to guide them in. Hurry up! We'll miss it." The two girls crawled together to their vantage point and took turns to look through the telescope as the drama played out beneath them.

The boat was the first to show a light. A green lantern was hoisted up the mast. After about a minute a single figure walked out onto the beach and held up a lantern in answer to the signal. Immediately, the boat altered course towards the shore, bringing the wind onto her beam.

"Someone's getting wet feet," Elaine whispered, her right eye glued to the telescope. The boat had very little freeboard and she could see the figures bailing frantically as the swell lapped at, and over, the gunwale. "They must be mad to try this!" Elaine said in some awe. Even the slightest shift in the wind or a single rogue wave would be very bad news for the boat and its crew.

"Um, I think we have more company coming in!" Lydia tugged Elaine's sleeve and pointed towards the route the first four figures had taken when they approached the beach. A small parade of lights twinkled in the dunes below them and to their left. Elaine turned the telescope towards the glittering snake.

"There must be twenty at least!" she said. "And Skelder hasn't more than twelve!"

"If there's too many, won't the militia just sit tight?" Lydia asked.

"Depends." Elaine's voice had grown serious. "Lydia, what if that creep has set your father up? This could be an ambush but not by the soldiers!"

"We could warn them!" Lydia saw Elaine shake her head in the darkness.

"Much too risky. Besides, we don't know what's really going on here. It could all be going to plan."

By now the boat was close inshore. The four figures on the beach moved towards the water's edge. The girls saw the sail come down just as the prow dug into the shelving sand. "Nice timing!" Elaine was ever admiring of good ship-handling. She handed the telescope to Lydia and concentrated on watching the boat. One of the figures in the boat jumped out and approached the man holding the lantern. They huddled together for a moment before each turned and signalled their colleagues.

A clearly well-rehearsed plan swung into action. The second party of men streamed out onto the beach and quickly formed a human chain passing boxes, crates and barrels out of the boat and rapidly along to where two small horse-drawn carts were waiting. The first cart was nearly full in no time and still the militia didn't stir from their hiding place in the dunes. "What's keeping them?" Elaine whispered impatiently. Lydia didn't reply. She was trying to focus on one of several men who were not helping to load the carts. He seemed to be holding something under his cloak.

"What's keeping them?" Thomas D'Shan hissed to Captain Skelder. The time was perfect for him to act. Unfortunately, a very important piece of the plan had not arrived. There was no sign of HMS Hunter. The plan had been for them to send in marines by boat to assist his men in the arrests. Time was slipping by. He needed to make a decision.

"There's too many of them, Sir," Skelder whispered. "Groth said no more than ten. There must be nearly thirty men out there!" Skelder's position was not as good as that occupied by the girls. From where he was half-crouched in the dune, it looked like there were an awful lot of men out there. "This one's a bust, sir. Without the marines we can't hope..."

"Captain!" Thomas fought the urge to grasp the man by the throat. "We have no option here! We must apprehend these people – or destroy them. You understand me? We cannot allow this raid to fail. Tell your men to volley fire then move in and arrest anyone they can. That is an order, Captain. Make it happen!" Skelder realised belatedly just how desperate Thomas D'Shan's position must be. He'd suspected that there was a lot more to this mission than he'd been told. It was, however, too late to worry about that now. Skelder had received his fair share of ill-conceived orders in his career but he knew that there was only one way to respond to them.

"Yes, Sir!"

From the vantage point on the ridge the events below appeared distant; like the moves in a chess game. Two groups of human figures were in position waiting for the cue to make their opening moves. A blue flare rose suddenly from the edge of the dunes and a shrill whistle sounded. The two small groups of militia stood and without warning or challenge fired a devastating volley at the line of men on the beach. Without pause, they lowered their muskets and ran down from the dunes towards the remaining smugglers. Their bayonets caught the moonlight as they ran.

Some confusion might have been expected. The smugglers had plenty of time to react and with the decent head start most could have fled. Instead the figures Lydia had been examining brought up muskets of their own from where they had been concealed beneath their cloaks. Those from the human chain who had not fallen from their wounds drew swords and cutlasses and turned to face the threat.

"Oh my!" Elaine and Lydia watched appalled as a terrible fight erupted on the beach beneath them. The soldiers initially had the best of it and at least three more smugglers fell before the bayonet charge. However, the numbers were not in their favour and once the smugglers organised themselves things began to go wrong. First one then another dark-coated figure was cut down. The militia faltered in the face of this determined resistance. With the loss of the initiative they were forced into a desperate fighting retreat as the tide of events turned against them. The smugglers took heart and pulled pistols from their belts. In a bloody exchange of fire, they inflicted five more deaths at the cost of only two of their own

Thomas D'Shan's rage at last had an outlet. He was engaged in a desperate fight with two men whose features had been blacked out with coal dust. Only their wild eyes caught the pale light, giving them a demonic appearance. They were strong and determined but Thomas was a good match; making up in skill and pure fury what he lacked in strength. To his left, Skelder was hard pressed but holding his own. To his right, four militiamen were being overrun. The situation was desperate but there was no option for either side but to to fight on. Thomas dealt what he judged to be a mortal blow to one of his opponents before an unexpected searing pain clouded his vision. He felt himself stumble and fall.

"The boat's getting away!" Elaine spotted the much lighter boat swinging free of the sand as figures battled frantically with the sail. Lydia was scanning the confused melee through the telescope.

"I can't make anybody out!" she said, her voice anguished. "I can see several bodies. Elaine, Father's down there!"

"He can take care of himself," Elaine said, in what she hoped was a convincing effort to reassure her cousin. "I think it's time we left." Elaine was trembling, though not from the cold. Despite reaching the conclusion that they should leave neither girl was able to tear themselves away. The scene had a ghastly hypnotic quality and both needed to know how it ended.

Abruptly, a deafening cacophony of sound rent the night overwhelming the sounds of fighting on the beach. The air was torn by sound like a giant knife ripping across the bay. Light flared from the twin rows of open gun ports as HMS HUNTER swept into the bay under full sail. The muzzle flash from the cannons illuminated two boats crammed full with marines rowing full tilt for the shore. The water around the small smuggling craft erupted into wild foam obscuring it from view but it emerged unscathed with sail set.

The smugglers realised in that instant that the game was up. Only one option – that of very rapid retreat - remained open to them and they seized upon it, breaking as one and running for the cover of the dunes. HUNTER's boats touched the beach and marines poured over the sides, running ashore as if taking part in a drill and forming rank.

What followed was the most appalling sight either girl had ever witnessed. The first row knelt, bringing their muskets up as they did so. The second row stood behind, their muskets also level. The volley was followed immediately by a second ragged broadside from the frigate. Stabs of flame burst vengefully from her hull lighting the beach at intervals which gave the figures below the appearance of moving in slow motion.

The sand around the feet of the retreating smugglers puffed up as most of the musket fire fell short. One smuggler, though, was hit. In the flashing of the canon fire Elaine saw his feet stumble. His arms flew up over his head which jerked backwards. His mouth was open in a cry that was drowned out by the man-made thunder in the bay before he fell headlong into the sand. Bravely, another figure retraced his steps and grabbed his fallen companion. With wild strength he dragged the limp form out of range as shot from the quickest of the marines fell about him. The still figure was loaded onto the empty cart and borne away with the surviving smugglers and all of the goods they had managed to load.

When the smoke cleared on the bay there was no sign of the smugglers' ship. There seemed to be quite a lot of debris bobbing on the swell where it had last been. HUNTER's sails were disappearing fast, like a swan folding her wings. The frigate lost way and turned her bow out towards the Cathe before dropping a single anchor. The beach was littered with human driftwood after the bloody storm. As the last echoes of gunfire died, the shouts and cries of the wounded begin to carry to the ridge behind the dunes.

Neither girl had ever thought to hear such anguish in the voices of grown men. The sound added a new ghastly horror to what had already been a thoroughly shocking experience for them. Grasped by a sudden desire to escape they helped each other back to the horses, stumbling as they did so. Tears coursed down their faces and their hands began to shake. Cries from the beach seemed to follow them back to Wescliffe on the wind.

Chapter Six - Enemies

A gentle cold wind stirred the bare branches of the trees and sent sparse white wisps of cloud scudding across the blue sky. Lydia watched the shapes drift by above her and relished the sweet smell of slightly damp grass and bracken.

To her left, Elaine was sprawled untidily across the rough scrub fast asleep. Her dark hair was loose and occasionally moved in the wind but Elaine herself was still. Two sleepless nights had finally caught up with her cousin and Lydia was glad to see her finally at peace. This was their first escape from Wescliffe since darkness had come to the house on the night of the raid. The injury to Lydia's father had lifted the ban on them leaving the house. He needed quiet to rest.

The events the girls had witnessed on the beach had been bad enough but nothing could have prepared them for the hellish scenes at Wescliffe when the wounded were brought there. The first had arrived scarcely twenty minutes after the girls had regained their beds without detection.

The surgeon from HMS HUNTER had turned the dining room into a makeshift hospital, pressing everyone into service in an attempt to save those (including Lydia's father) deemed not beyond hope. Perhaps surprisingly, the blood and suffering had affected Elaine to a much greater extent than Lydia. After the first nightmare hour, the death of Hicks under the surgeon's knife had proved too much. Lydia's mother, glad perhaps of the excuse, had taken the shaking and sobbing Elaine to her room.

Lydia had remained to the last tortured moment. By the end the blood had scarcely affected her at all. The screams as the surgeon had amputated the sergeant's shattered leg had been the worst trial of her nerve.

At first, she had believed her father dead. He had been so still and pale when he was brought in that it seemed beyond doubt. However, the surgeon had hopes for him, barring infection, though with the loss of blood and depth of the wound he would take a very long time to recover.

Lydia turned her head to check that the horses had not wandered too far before gazing again at the sky. The events of the past two days had passed in a blur, not allowing those caught up in them much time for reflection. Now, in the solitude of the moment, Lydia began to piece together her emotions and fears more coherently.

At the forefront of her consciousness were the raw emotions of the trauma she had suffered. The first thing she had seen on the morning following the raid had been bodies lined up in the front yard. A row of canvas hammocks, sewn up navy fashion, were now awaiting burial. She had never expected to witness such a grisly scene at Wescliffe.

The next layer of her emotions were more subtle but much stronger. Scraps of overheard conversation led her to believe that the disaster was of a personal magnitude surpassing the terrible loss of life (and failure to seize a single piece of contraband). It had implications for her father's job. Already several junior servants were becoming insolent, which could only mean that they expected a change of master. What could this mean for her, Lydia wondered. Might it mean leaving the island? That was a thought almost too terrible to contemplate yet it hung over her like an unresolved threat.

Then there was the worry about whether her father would make a swift and full recovery. She knew the risk of infection was very great but she worried more about his spirit. If he was indeed facing ruin, might he just lose the will to live? The outcome of the previous night's events could yet be fatal and she was helpless to alter it.

Lydia's attempt to bring resolution to her fears failed. She eventually fell into a fretful sleep beside Elaine leaving the stoic horses to their own devices. They spotted a distant figure approaching at a brisk walk but, being horses, disregarded it as irrelevant and continued with their grazing.

The wild scrubland beneath the escarpment of the high ground, at the centre of the island, was a harsh landscape of coarse grass. This was cropped short by grazing ponies, sheep and cattle. Their owners exercised the ancient right to keep these and other animals on what was common land. Scattered about the landscape were patches of wild gorse that offered the only available shelter. Many of these clumps were to be found around the innumerable shallow dells which dotted the landscape; scars of the island's earliest forays into quarrying the granite stone from which most of the island's buildings were constructed.

The girls had chosen to come here today mainly because they were too tired for a longer ride. Groth had chosen it because it was conveniently close to Wescliffe, the source of his present troubles.

If things had gone badly for Thomas D'Shan, they had gone doubly so for Groth. His scheming had backfired in the worst possible way. Clearly those he had set up had suspected something was amiss and had brought reinforcements along. D'Shan now suspected him of double-dealing and had barred him from the house. This had brought a sudden and unwelcome end to his financial arrangements. About the only ray of good fortune was that Groth knew the two most dangerous smugglers who had suspected him had disappeared – permanently – with their boat into the Cathe.

His position now was particularly uncomfortable. Money was owed on his gambling debts. D'Shan had cut him off and the nastiest of Groth's contacts, the receivers of the goods, were wondering where their contraband was. Frankly, Groth was wondering the same. Not so much as a bottle of mediocre wine had been seized, yet a full cart-load of merchandise was still unaccounted for. His contact wanted that merchandise and if it was not found quickly then Groth's own life would be in danger.

It was with this complex and dark mixture of thoughts that Groth struck out across the Downs. He was dwelling on the particular risk to his life when he came suddenly upon a sheltered dell with two sleeping forms in it. He halted and stared in surprised recognition for an instant before rapidly asking himself whether this might be an opportunity to acquire some life insurance.

There were two of them and one of him but he would have the advantage of surprise. So which, Groth asked himself, was the most useful to him? The answer to that was obvious.

Stealth came as naturally to Groth as swimming did to most people of Wrea. With swift, catlike movements he crossed over to the horses and removed a coil of rope from behind the saddle of the chestnut mare. His movements became more deliberate and quieter still as he crept towards the sleeping girls. Like a hungry spider, he crouched over Elaine before pouncing. In an instant he clamped one hand roughly across her face. His other hand grasped her left arm and twisted it behind her back in a single vicious movement.

Elaine awoke in terror from a disturbed dream world into a nightmare reality. Disoriented, unable to move and in pain, she wriggled like an eel but Groth's full weight bore down on her preventing escape. The pain in her arm as he twisted it further quelled the fight within her in a haze of agony. She felt rope about her wrists tighten until it was digging into her flesh. Something cold and sharp pricked the skin of her neck just below her left ear.

"Not a sound Miss Elaine, if you please. You scream or struggle I'll gut you like a herring on your father's boat, you understand?" Elaine's eyes met his and though she didn't acknowledge him, Groth decided she understood well enough. The rough hand came off her face. Elaine was rolled onto her front and her feet tied. She turned her head. Lydia lay a short distance away, still asleep. In an instant, the memory of Lydia's hand on her arm in the art room at school came to mind; the feeling of being pulled back by a friend from a dark place.

"LYDIA! RUN!" The scream tore from her throat unbidden in response to the memory. With a terrible curse, Groth threw himself at Lydia but he was not quick enough to catch her feet. On instinct Lydia had rolled away from the scream, waking as she did so. Out of the corner of her eye she saw a shape lunging at her and so pulled her feet away from Groth's outstretched hands. Lydia screamed, scrabbling away and to her feet as Groth picked himself up. "RUN! GO!" Elaine's words were both a command and a desperate plea. Groth was far more of a danger to Lydia than her, Elaine felt. She wanted her friend safe. Lydia turned and ran towards the horses. Groth half started to follow before he turned suddenly and bore down on Elaine.

The scream halted Lydia in her tracks. Groth had hauled Elaine to her feet by her hair and now held a hunting knife to her throat.

"Not another step, Miss Lydia. Let's be thoughtful about this, shall we? I don't need to hurt your friend if you do what you're told. Now come over here." Elaine saw the look in Lydia's eyes and began to weep. Her cousin would not leave her any more than she would leave Lydia. Lydia's cheeks were also tear-stained as she did what she was told. Unlike Elaine, who felt she was being used to put her friend in danger, Lydia's were tears of impotent rage. Groth's face bore a smug look of triumph as he ordered Lydia back. He roughly bound her hands and feet. Lydia felt a tide of hatred and fury swell within her. All she could do in response was spit in his face, for which she received a vicious slap in return.

Groth brought his face close to Lydia's and held her chin, his dirty nails digging into her cheek. He stared into her eyes and once again a sort of hypnotic terror came over her. The sun went suddenly behind a dark cloud, or so it seemed to her. She felt small and vulnerable in front of some large menacing terror. This sense of confusion grew until, with a short unnatural scream, she passed out allowing Groth to sling her over the horse.

Elaine watched in appalled silence. She sensed the enchantment at work on her friend as a black mist flowing from Groth to Lydia like a semi-visible poison. At once she felt the same sudden surge of apprehension that had preceded her first meeting with the man. Her emotions switched suddenly from misery to anger. Unlike Lydia, Elaine sensed that somewhere within her lay the power to unlock this anger. As she watched Groth turn from Lydia and approach her she desperately searched for the means to release that power. Groth stood over her and spoke in a satisfied mocking tone.

"Now, Miss Elaine, I don't doubt that an intelligent lass like yourself will be free of those ties before too long. I'll be taking Lydia here with me, you see? Now, you're to be a good little girl and run back to Wescliffe to give Lydia's father the good news, right? I'll be needing money, but he knows that! Mostly what I need is to find out where all my merchandise has gone. He needs to find that out for me; not too hard for a Revenue Officer I'd have thought! I'll want about three hundred crowns to start with. I'll give him a day or so to arrange that and then I'll be in touch about where to drop the money off." Groth's voice took on a more menacing tone when he continued. "Of course, any messing about and this will be the last time you see Lydia alive. I need my merchandise. If he can't deliver, I'll be wanting a lot more gold."

Groth smiled, enjoying a sadistic moment of triumph. "I'm a reasonable man, so I'll leave him enough of his fortune that he can bury his daughter in style, should that become necessary. Here's a little something to help you remember the message."

Groth's boot stamped down hard on Elaine's right ankle, causing a burst of pain down into her foot and all the way up her spine. Satisfied with the cry of pain and renewed tears, Groth turned and led the horse carrying Lydia away.

"HELP!" Elaine's voice was weak from shouting yet the cry came from her heart and was still loud enough to carry some distance if only there were someone to hear. Not that she had confined herself merely to shouting. After much wriggling she had come across a rock that might serve to cut through the rope about her wrists. Groth had bound her hands so tightly that she quickly did as much damage to her own skin as the rope. She felt warm blood trickle through her clenched fingers. "HELP!" All her rage and desperation went into a final cry before Elaine fell silent. Desperately she worked rope against rock while her teeth were clenched against the pain. There was no-one to hear, she thought, so why waste the effort of shouting?

In the centre of the Cathe a sleek two-masted schooner was heading Sor towards Perth Cathe under full sail. A solitary robed figure rested easily on the starboard gunwale looking across to Thirnmar's distant shoreline which gleamed silver in the sunlight. Despite a number of sailors going about their business, the figure was alone. It was as if he was surrounded by an invisible aura that no-one entered. By time-honoured custom of the sea, the Captain's side of the quarterdeck was his alone to enjoy. TEOCEROMO's motion was easy in a light swell and the figure moved gracefully in time with it, seemingly at one with both ship and sea.

Abruptly, he turned with a look of horror on his face. He fairly leaped across to the port side, much to the alarm of several sailors who hastily made themselves scarce. Daren Berant stared across to Fain-Arn, reaching out with his mind to catch again a call that had broken sharply into his thoughts. He heard it again, only once. A plea filled with pain, despair and fear.

"HELM! HARD APORT!" His voice was laden with such rage that for an instant the sailors hesitated before jumping to the sheets. Yards creaked around and canvas cracked loudly across as TEOCEROMO turned sharply into the wind. Daren leaned far out over the side and his voice roared out in a strange tongue. The turn had brought TEOCEROMO's head into the wind but as the last syllables of his voice died so did the wind. A new breeze sprang up, strong and true from the Wes. TEOCEROMO forged ahead. To a few astonished sailors aboard nearby vessels she appeared to gather speed, sailing directly into the wind.

Daren had not finished yet however. Again his voice cried out. At his command a distant speck, far away near the island of Elledran, ceased its search for food and began to move purposefully towards Fain-Arn.

Elaine had to rest. The effort required to work the rope against a rock was considerable. The pain in her wrists by this time was almost unbearable. She closed her eyes. Her breath came in short gasps as she tried to muster the will to try again.

She heard a noise; close by. Suddenly Elaine was still. Fearing that she knew who it was, she mustered all her energy to struggle and scream if he so much as touched her. But it was not a man who had disturbed the heather behind her and now hopped lightly into view. Elaine found herself meeting the unblinking yellow stare of an Aethmar. These were large birds, something between an albatross and the smaller fish eating eagles of inland waters. Rare and as wild as the sea over which they lived, Elaine had never heard tell of one being seen on Fain-Arn.

The bird's feathers were mostly white with flecks of grey and a spread of black at each wing tip. Its feet were not webbed but clawed with the strength to seize a large fish from the water and carry it in flight. Its beak was sharp and curved. The Aethmar stared at her, not moving at all.

Understanding was slow to dawn. Even when it did, Elaine could not tell from where it came or how. Suddenly she realised what she had to do. She rolled onto her side and held herself completely still as the Aethmar hopped closer and inspected the bloody mess with keen eyes. His attack on the rope was quick and precise like a surgeon's lancet. Three sharp tugs and the rope slackened before falling away. Elaine's hands, though now free, were swollen and painful. The Aethmar was obliged to work on the rope about her ankles as well. After he had done so he hopped back as Elaine scrambled to her feet.

Casting quickly about her, Elaine saw that Groth had not taken her horse. She must have lain bound for nearly twenty minutes but if he were on foot that would not be so bad; if only she could tell where he had gone. Clearly Groth had assumed she would ride straight to Wescliffe for help. Elaine was not about to abandon her cousin whatever Groth might think. She turned to the Aethmar.

"Thank you. My friend, a man took her; on a horse. Can you show me?" The rational part of her mind recoiled from the fact that she was talking to a sea bird, yet some other part was not surprised at all when with a shrill cry the Aethmar leapt upwards. Its huge powerful wings hauled it up to the currents and thermals it was used to.

Elaine climbed painfully onto her horse and watched the Aethmar soar higher and higher until it was just a small dot. Suddenly its cry rang out once again across the island, distant but distinct. The dot wheeled and glided Nor-Est. "Long Forn!" muttered Elaine. The logic was sound. Groth was making for the nearest large area of woodland Nor of the high ground at the centre of the island. A good place to hide but it was some distance and Elaine was sure they would not be there yet. She spurred the horse to a reckless gallop and followed the line the bird was taking.

At sea, the TEOCEROMO was now within two miles of Fain-Arn's coast. To their Nor, barely visible, were the wharves and buildings of Perth Calran. Daren ordered a change of course towards it and instructed the crew to anchor in the outer part of the harbour until his return. It was his intention to be ashore before they got there.

Groth had been making fairly brisk progress during this time but was not in any particular hurry. The undulating nature of the terrain and patchy gorse protected him from being seen from any great distance – at least from the direction of Wescliffe where any pursuit would originate. He fully expected Elaine to remain bound for at least two hours, maybe even until the following morning when a search party would no doubt find her. He increased his pace to a jog only when approaching the rough track, well pitted with the passage of carts, from Harton to Perth Calran.

Before crossing, Groth led the horse into a dell and tied it securely with its precious cargo. Stealthily he then made his way, crouching low, to a bush at the side of the track. He scanned the horizon in both directions to check that the way was clear. Only when satisfied did he make a dash for it. He eased off his pace again as soon as the road was hidden from view by a slight ridge.

The landscape was more open and wild now. The grass and occasional scrub gave way to inhospitable moorland, as it climbed towards the higher ground at the island's centre. The way ahead was dotted with large granite boulders through which he had to pick a route suitable for the horse. He would have to make brisk time to minimise the risk of being seen out in the open, though he judged there was no-one likely to be out here. He used what cover he could find but favoured speed above caution. Lydia was awake again and wept as she was jostled and jolted. Her tears had no effect on Groth. Misery was something he inflicted as a matter of course and no amount of distress would move his cold heart.

Groth was not an aesthetic man. The world had no particular beauty for him, except in the form of negotiable coins and paper notes. He was not a man to enjoy the fine sunsets for which the islands of Thirnmar were famed; nor was he in the habit of noticing anything about his surroundings that was not immediately relevant to his needs. Thus he did not even register the presence of a circling bird high above his head as he trudged purposefully towards the dense woodland of Long Forn about a mile away at the top of the uneven rock-strewn slope. Equally importantly, he was also unaware of a figure just within the trees who watched his approach keenly from the back of a jet-black horse.

This figure was shaded, sitting just to one side of a shaft of sunlight which fell through the bare branches above to create a mottled patchwork on leaves about him. His back was straight and a hand came up to his brow as he gazed intently at the landscape below. The figure leading a horse had been under observation for some time. Long enough to draw the conclusion that the odd shape on the back of the horse he was leading must be a body.

This by itself was enough of a mystery to merit close attention but he leaned forwards in eager anticipation when he spied movement in the distance by the track they had recently crossed. The distant speck resolved itself into the shape of a small rider who seemed to be in pursuit. The black horse was edged closer to the edge of the trees and its master leaned forwards in anticipation as the pursuer drew closer to the man on foot and appeared to ride right at him.

Groth was slow to respond to the sudden reappearance of Elaine, which was to the good. Whether through his preoccupation or a trick of the wind he only heard the hooves when it was almost too late. Elaine spurred her horse recklessly in a determined effort to trample him. A desperate leap saved Groth's life (he remained lucky he thought). Elaine reined in her mount hard. She spun around to try again but now she lacked the advantage of speed and surprise. Groth was able to sidestep and pluck her from the saddle. Elaine fell heavily and painfully onto the rocky ground where she lay stunned for a moment.

The man in the tree line watched the mini battle come to a premature end with some disappointment. "My, my." His voice was soft, almost musical. "Tcheh!" he urged his own horse forward out of the trees before breaking into an easy canter towards the small group. "What might we have here?" he mused.

Groth was enraged to a point he had never reached before. By nature a cold man, this was a new experience but then so was the persistent defiance of the girl now in his iron grip. Even now, with death staring maliciously at her, he saw defiance in her eyes.

"You young fool!" The words tumbled almost incoherently from his mouth. "It's death you want is it? Well it's yours, but don't expect it to be quick." The knife was in his hands and he was about to use it when a voice called out from close by.

"Ho! What do you think you are about? Unhand the lady this instant!" A young man was close by on a jet-black horse which, it seemed, had made no sound during its approach. The rider sprang to the ground and his right hand rested lightly on the silver hilt of a sword about his waist. He matched Groth in height but little could be seen of his features beneath the hood of the cloak.

"She's no lady but a thief!" Groth snarled, irritated by this second unwelcome intrusion. "No better than the friend she's trying to help. They're both wanted by the militia to meet an appointment with the gallows. It's the King's business I'm on, young Master, so you'd best leave me to it."

"Liar!" Elaine spat the word. "Sir, that is Lydia D'Shan. This man is a kidnapper and a blackmailer. It is he who should hang!"

"Silence wench!" The back of Groth's hand sent Elaine tumbling again to the ground. "Lies, master. Filthy lies from a gutter bitch."

"Not so fast there, sir." The young man's tone took on an edge of command. "These girls are not dressed as thieves, dirty though their clothes are. Let me see the one on the horse." As he spoke he drew a slender sword.

"Don't be deceived by her appearance young man," Groth answered, forcing himself to appear calm as he lifted Lydia's face for inspection by pulling her hair. "These clothes were stolen from Wescliffe not two days ago."

"I think not." The young man took a couple of steps forward as Groth let Lydia's head fall. "Step away, sir, or it will go badly for you." The command was calm and assured.

"That I cannot do young Master." Groth moved around and placed himself between the girls and the man. He fixed the would-be rescuer with a hard stare as he concentrated his will.

The man's reaction surprised him. He sheathed his sword and stepped back in surprise but without fear.

"So that's your game is it?" he enquired. Genuine amusement sounded in his voice. "I pity you for a fool." The man swept his cloak back over his shoulders and dropped the hood. He was very well dressed in a fine tunic. The silver sword hung from a jewelled belt. Rings of silver adorned several fingers. His face was slender with high cheek bones and a strong jaw. There was a determined set to his mouth and the dark eyes that bore into Groth's own and betrayed a will of iron. About his neck was a thick chain from which hung a red gem in the shape of a three-pointed crown. With a cry of fear, Groth shrank back. "You would try a hag's enchantment on the Kashaan Eed would you?" The young man's voice rang now with anger and menace in an abrupt change from his former tone. Darkness seemed to gather about him as he spoke.

"Forgive me, I did not realise. Have the girls. They are worth something I assure you." The words tumbled quickly from Groth's mouth in an effort to save himself.

"Well I know it!" The man replied. "That you have the audacity to even look at them displeases me! Who are you to threaten my kin? You are nothing but a sneak, a cutpurse, and a luckless gambler; a thug, and a worker of feeble enchantments without the wit to understand that which he does!" A bolt of darkness sprang from the man's hands and struck Groth full in the chest, hurling him several feet away to where he landed and lay motionless.

Elaine watched the man come across to Lydia and untie her before helping her down from the horse. The sense of evil Elaine got from their "rescuer" far surpassed that which she got from Groth. He held Lydia a moment while she steadied herself, rubbing life back into her wrists and ankles.

"Thank you." Lydia was confused and disoriented. She had not seen all of what had passed between the man and Groth, but naturally regarded the man as a rescuer. Elaine was not so sure.

"Do not thank me, cousin," the man replied. "Who is he to threaten you? My, Lydia, you are quite the young lady! I doubt Aunt Catherine will be too pleased about the state of your dress, though." Lydia recoiled from his grasp.

"Tristan?" It was both a question and a gasp of fear.

"Did you not recognise me? I am hurt!" Tristan spoke lightly, as if in jest, yet every word carried a dark threat underneath. "I suppose I have changed; as have you! I am come into my power, cousin. I am Kashaan Eed, a "dark mage" as some simple fools would have it. The King has still not seen fit to install a mage on Fain-Arn, I find. Well, his loss is to be my gain. I am back, cousin, and this time I intend to stay. Good news, don't you think?" Lydia nodded weakly, taking another step back.

"We should be getting back." Elaine spoke for the first time.

"No doubt you should," Tristan replied. "But fool though he was, poor Mr Groth was not wrong. You are valuable and I have need of you. Perhaps my father can be persuaded to step aside without his weak heart giving out on him. No, my dear girls, you will be coming with me."

"No, Tristan!" Lydia turned and ran to her horse, suddenly desperately afraid.

"Lydia! You could not resist the bewitchment of a fool. Do you think I cannot make you do as I command?" Tristan waved a hand and the two horses reared in panic and fled. Elaine and Lydia huddled fearfully together.

"We will not go with you!" Elaine said, her voice trembled but a sudden resolve burned within her. Enough was enough.

"Brave words from your friend, Lydia." Tristan smiled. "Very well, let us see how strong you are!"

The enchantment, which was of an altogether darker sort than the one Groth had used, struck Elaine without warning like a physical force that dropped her to her knees. The emotions it stirred within her were a mixture of fear and despair. It was as though Tristan were inside her head, willing her to give in to desire for a sleep from which there would be no awakening. Dark forms lurked, the half-visions of the dreams that would haunt her and yet was that not preferable to the terrible weight of the struggle?

Elaine fought him. She fought the drowsiness; refusing to give in, though the torture of the effort was like nothing she had ever experienced. Every fibre of her being rebelled against it. She drew ever deeper from a strength she had not known she possessed but of which she knew she had little left. The struggle lasted what seemed a lifetime, though it was perhaps as little as thirty seconds when:

"Enough!" A stern voice broke the enchantment abruptly. Elaine collapsed against her cousin, gasping for breath. Lydia held her tightly and looked up to see the last man she had expected. The Mageseeker who had saved them at the school stood before them once again, dressed now in a pale blue robe and clasping a slender staff tipped with white horn. His blue eyes were locked on Tristan and a terrible rage and strength emanated from him.

"What business is this of yours, mage?" Tristan asked sullenly, stepping back as if from a light too bright for his eyes.

"I do not share my business with the likes of you, Tristan D'Shan!" Daren snapped. "These girls are known to me. That is enough. Did you think that the King would let you return to Fain-Arn unopposed? You are henceforth under sentence of banishment from the kingdom. Wheldor, too, is closed to you!"

"I do not choose to recognise this banishment," Tristan replied hotly. "Do you think you can defeat me seawitch?" As he spoke, darkness gathered once again about him and the girls shrank away.

"You will leave," Daren replied calmly. "You have no choice."

Tristan opened his arms and uttered a string of incomprehensible syllables. His voice rang with power and the harsh language seemed to stain the very air with evil. There was a terrible sound, like the tearing of some giant fabric. A dark shape swirled and solidified between him and Daren. Darkness flowed about it like viscous liquid. Evil seeped from it into the ground, shrivelling the grass and causing nearby gorse to writhe and wither. Terror swam about it, stifling the breath in the girls' lungs. The shape lunged at Daren.

As it did so, white light burst from the tip of his staff. Intensely bright to the point of pain, the girls turned their eyes away hastily. They did not see the light intensify further, consuming the creature as if in flame. They heard a shrill unnatural cry from Tristan that stopped abruptly. The light faded and he, along with the creature, was gone. Daren appeared untouched and unruffled. With the threat gone he was once again the quiet, slender, unassuming character the girls had first met at the school. All trace of anger and power had gone from his bearing. They now understood him better, however. This calm authority came from real power that was hidden, like a sheathed sword, but real and dangerous nonetheless.

"Come," Daren said calmly. "Let's get you home." He led the girls gently away and neither noticed that the place where Groth had fallen earlier was now unoccupied.

Chapter Seven - Escape

A search party was about to set out from Wescliffe when the girls and their guide finally dragged their weary feet through the gate. Daren and Lydia were supporting Elaine and were grateful when the servants rushed into the yard to assist them. Willing hands whisked Elaine up to her room where a fire was quickly laid for her.

The horses had returned rider-less and this had caused quite a stir. Thomas D'Shan, mindful of the recent implied threat to Lydia's safety, had been in the process of mobilising the island's entire militia garrison. Riders were hastily sent to Perth Cathe and Perth Calran to rescind the call-out order.

The girls were cold and exhausted. In Lydia's case this was partly due to Groth's enchantment. In Elaine's it had more to do with the battle of wills with Tristan, or so she thought. Lydia was discharged to the care of the Housekeeper along with orders to get both girls to bed with something hot to drink before they went to sleep. Daren then made his way to the day room to speak to Thomas.

Thomas had heard of Daren Berant, but had never thought to find himself facing the man. Daren had a reputation as a powerful Weatherworker and a rather stern character. The second part was soon confirmed. Daren fixed Thomas with a very hard stare.

"Mr D'Shan, I had the good fortune to rescue your daughter and niece from a very nasty situation today," Daren began without preamble. "You will appreciate, I'm sure, that little passes on this island that I do not know about. Your arrangement with the smugglers was foolish and dangerous. It has placed your daughter at risk and probably ruined you! The last is your own affair and it concerns me not. However, as if that were not enough, Tristan D'Shan has returned to the island. In fact, it was from him that I rescued the girls since he had already driven that Groth fellow away with something to remember him by. I am confident that Tristan will leave the island. He is no match for me and he knows it. Until that time, however, he poses a further threat to your family. I suggest you consider getting them to a place of safety until Groth is arrested and Tristan removed."

Not many people could have spoken to Thomas in this way. Only a few days previously even Daren would have received a firm rebuff but Thomas's spirits had fallen low. His wound sent pain coursing through his body, though he hid the fact well. In addition, he had been consumed with fear for the girl's safety and this crushing terror had not yet fully passed. As a result, Daren's curt analysis of Thomas's ill-considered dealings with Groth cut deeply; the worse for their moral authority and truth.

Thomas's emotions were so numbed that the thanks Daren might have expected for saving the girls was not forthcoming. Thomas was grateful - more so than he could ever express - but he could no more communicate that emotion now than he could restore his own reputation and honour.

"My wife can go to Thirnmar," Thomas replied, his head bowed. "We received a letter today asking Elaine to go home. Her father has been taken ill it seems."

"Then send Lydia to TolSor with her," Daren ordered in a tone that did not bear argument. "You would perhaps do well to cross to Thirnmar also. The danger to your daughter would be much diminished if you did so."

"No!" Thomas's voice took on something of its old tone, albeit muted by pain and exhaustion. "I will not run like a whipped dog! I have my duty still, until I am relieved of it."

"You are late indeed to begin thinking of duty," the mage replied dryly. "How you attend to your own skin is your business. Perhaps it would be as well to see things through. I caution you, however, to tell no-one where the girls are and keep good guard here at the house. I will attend to Tristan. The threat that is of your own making is beyond my authority to deal with."

"I shall take care of that," Thomas assured his guest.

"Very well. In the meantime, see that you drink two drops of this morning and night. It will preserve your wounds from infection." Daren took a small phial from a pouch at his waist and set it on the table. "With your permission, I shall take my leave. I will return in the morning to give your wife passage to Thirnmar and give physic to the girls. See that they are not disturbed in the meantime. Sleep is the best cure at present. I shall treat the more obvious injuries tomorrow when they have greater strength but for tonight they need sleep above all else."

"It shall be as you say," Thomas assured his guest. His wife, he was sure, would want to apply all manner of poultices and treatments. Thomas decided to remind her that Master Berant was known to have treated the King himself. Whilst she had little time for Mages and spell-craft, Mrs D'Shan had the utmost respect for anyone associated with Court.

Before he turned in for the night, Thomas scribbled a hasty note to Elaine's mother, confirming that Elaine would be sent home as soon as possible and saying that Lydia would be coming with her. It was something of an imposition but from what contact he had previously had with Elaine's parents it was one he knew he could count on. A trusted servant was dispatched immediately for Perth Cathe from where the letter would be taken on to Tol Sor.

Daren returned early the next day. He spoke briefly to Mrs D'Shan about the need for haste and bringing the minimum amount of baggage possible. He then ascended the stairs and knocked first on Lydia's door.

"Come in." Lydia was confined to her bed on the orders of her mother. For once, she was happy to comply. She felt weak and her dreams, when she had fallen into a restless sleep, were not the sort to bring comfort or rest. Daren entered the room and pulled up a chair at her bedside.

"How are you feeling?" he asked gently.

"Not too good sir, to tell you the truth," Lydia admitted. The dark rings under her eyes confirmed the fact.

"You are strong and will soon recover," Daren assured her. "The enchantment cast upon you was nasty but not particularly potent."

"What did Groth do, sir?" Lydia asked. Somehow this mage seemed a lot less intimidating here in her room than he had at either of their previous meetings.

"There are two sorts of magic in the world, child," Master Berant explained carefully. "We of the Kerun Dur use the power of light. It is light which binds the three worlds; Aiere, Erath and our own, Wrea, together. Light flows through each world as a binding force, linking them so that we may travel between them. It is light which created matter in the Void. Ours is the power to create. There are those who shun the light. They draw their power from the Void and theirs is the power to unmake. Some can manipulate the negative emotions such as fear, despair, hatred and anger. It was an enchantment of that type that Groth used on you and which Tristan attempted on your cousin. Groth uses the Void, as does your cousin Tristan. You would do well to choose the path of light, Lydia, lest you be led to the same dark place your cousin was. Tristan is Kashaan Eed. A Void Mage. He is powerful but arrogant and it is likely that his own power will consume him in time."

"I thought I didn't have the Gift," Lydia said, puzzled by the warning.

"My dear girl we all possess the Gift to some extent. Yours is a Lesser Gift, but it is a power nonetheless. Mr Groth has no more power than you do but he has turned that which he possesses to a dark purpose. The Kerun Dur takes only those with the Greater Gift and the very few, like Elaine, with the True Gift. We do so because such power is dangerous in the hands of those untrained to use it. They can bring about their own ruin or, worse still, be seduced by the Die Kashaan Eed and turn their power to darkness.

I sensed at the school that Elaine's path lay not to the Kerun Dur by a direct route. She will go there someday but her spirit is tied to water and so she shall take the first steps here on Wrea. It may be that you choose to accompany her on those first steps. You have remarkable courage and spirit, my girl. Your friend will need that. The True Gift is burdensome at times." A brief shadow crossed Daren's face as he said this but its passing was momentary. "That is the future and not the present. For now, be at peace and rest. The darkness shall not find you again." The mage stood and briefly placed his hand on Lydia's head. He removed it only when she had slipped into a deep and healing sleep free from the dreams that had previously tormented her. Daren watched her for a couple of minutes, much troubled in his own mind. Occasionally, as with Elaine at the school, he could sense something of the future. In Lydia's future he sensed change and uncertainty. More immediately, he sensed danger. With a sigh, Daren turned and made his way to Elaine's room.

He found Elaine in a worse state just as he had feared. She was running a fever and very weak. Elaine tried to sit up to greet him but was unable to. She ached all over and couldn't muster the strength to haul herself upright. She settled back into the pillow with a pained gasp.

"My dear child, be still," Master Berant commanded gently. "You have spent yourself. Your gift is great but you cannot use it without cost. You fought hard with Tristan as well as summoning my help. Do not seek to use your power again for a while. You must recover fully."

"How..." Elaine had so many questions but he silenced her gently with a wave of his hand.

"You felt the power within you, did you not? You then used it to fight the dark mage's enchantment. And you won. You have the True Gift, Elaine. Very few have such potential as you but it is dangerous to use that which you cannot control. There is a place you can go to learn this; closer than the Kerun Dur. You remember what I told you at the school?"

"Yours is the harder course to steer," Elaine answered weakly.

"Indeed, so it is," the man responded, "but not impossible. Trust your instincts, Elaine, particularly when you are at sea. Your soul is tied to water. The Sea Sprite sensed this when he gave you that." Daren nodded towards the flute on the table. "Rest and be at peace. Lydia is safe and will soon be her usual self. She owes you much."

"She tried to help me at the school," Elaine explained.

"She did," Master Berant agreed. "In truth, I have never seen such a thing. You have repaid that debt in full. Your friendship shall be all the stronger because of it. Now, let me attend to your hurts. You have been most badly treated." Elaine could not argue with that. Her ankle was swollen and throbbing relentlessly. Her wrists were in a fearful state and her face was bruised and puffy.

Daren attended to each with great care and considerable tenderness. He applied a poultice and bandage to her ankle before washing her wrists gently with ice cold water from a silver flask. He poured more water onto a cloth which he placed against her bruised face. During these activities he appeared to be quietly speaking in an unfamiliar tongue. There was a lilting, almost hypnotic, quality to it which brought to mind the Sea Sprite she had met at Perth Cathe. Finally, after about half an hour, Daren ordered Elaine to drink a small glass of the water before placing his hand on her head and sending her into a healing sleep as he had done Lydia.

When he left Wescliffe Master Berant took Mrs D'Shan with him. She could be heard complaining bitterly at the short notice and the fact that she had only been allowed a single trunk and a bag.

Thomas watched his wife leave with a heavy heart. Although theirs was not a particularly loving marriage he regretted her going; the more so because his heart told him that Wescliffe was not likely to be their home for much longer.

He turned suddenly from the window and with a strong curse swept the clutter on his desk to the floor with a loud crash. The desk received two thumps before the pain abated his temper. Stunned, he stared at the mess before silently turning his back on it and returning to the day room to reflect bitterly on his misfortune.

The girls' enchanted sleep lasted a full twenty-four hours. When they awoke, neither Lydia or Elaine could recall ever feeling so refreshed though both were very hungry. Elaine's injuries had healed to a remarkable extent. Only her wrists now required bandages.

The news that they were to leave Wescliffe was not much of a surprise and neither girl particularly minded. Elaine was naturally concerned about her father but these periods of illness were nothing new. The prospect of spending a week or so at home before returning to Harton was not unwelcome.

For her part, Lydia was also pleased. As Daren had predicted, both girls felt a friendship for each other that went far deeper than the alliance they had formed at school against Mary Newton and her crowd. They knew they could rely on each other under any circumstances and if Elaine needed to go home, then Lydia was perfectly willing to go with her. Of course, life at TolSor was likely to be different to what Lydia was used to, but she would adapt. After all, Elaine had made the effort to fit in at Wescliffe (corsets and all) and, for all her privileged upbringing, Lydia was not a lazy girl. The prospect of working the beacon tower did not worry her although she did feel some anxiety about how much use she would be. Willingness alone would not be much good if she was not up to the job.

"How are we to get there?" Lydia asked her father. "Might the road be watched?"

"If it is, I fail to see what we can do about it," Thomas replied. "I will of course send an escort with you. You will be well protected."

"Excuse me, sir," Elaine said thoughtfully. "If Master Berant wants Lydia hidden, that's not a very good way to do it. We'd be better going by sea. We can slip out of the bay at night and sail down the coast. You could also send a guarded carriage to the school. We won't be in it, but it will appear that you've sent us back to school early."

"I don't see how that's safer," Thomas objected mildly. "Surely at sea you'd be more vulnerable?" Lydia smiled.

"That's because you've never sailed the boat, Father. I doubt there's a faster vessel than SKYLARK within miles of here. Even if we're seen, we can outrun anything else afloat. Elaine's a fantastic sailor. We'd be much safer going by sea I promise you!" Neither girl added that having SKYLARK would give them a lot more freedom at the end of their journey. Lydia's father considered the plan, particularly the decoy coach. He needed Groth to tip his hand in order that he could move decisively against him. This, he thought, might be the way to do achieve that.

"Very well. You must leave tonight, as will the coach. ALBERT!" Thomas summoned one of the men servants before hastily scribbling a few lines. "Deliver this to Skelder in Perth Cathe. Now, girls, forgive me. This damned wound leaves me feeling so weak. I must rest."

The remainder of the day was taken up with preparation. The girls had much to pack, since it was not expected that Lydia would return to Wescliffe but go on to school from TolSor when the new term started. Elaine had a single small trunk which represented most of her worldly belongings. It was with some relief that she closed the drawer having left the borrowed corset inside. There was no use for it at TolSor and she had no intention at all of wearing it at school.

By mid-afternoon their trunks were lined up in the hallway ready to be carried out under cover of darkness. Under normal circumstances, both girls would have most certainly gone for a last ride over the downs but neither wanted to do so today. It would be a while until they took pleasure in that activity again. Lydia spent quite a while in her room staring blankly out of her window while she tried to make sense of the situation and her feelings about what the future might hold. This proved to be a fruitless exercise but it did at least allow her to drift into a short sleep which would no doubt prove useful later.

Elaine spent most of her time in the boathouse with SKYLARK. Canvas covers had to be removed again and the pleasure gained from revealing SKYLARK's sleek hull was scarcely less than on the first occasion. This time she was far more thorough. Sails were brought up and made ready. Ropes and halliards were checked for any weakness or fraying. Finally, a good deal of oil was used on the door hinges and windlass. Once she was satisfied that all was as ready as it could be, Elaine returned to the house to snatch a short sleep of her own.

Both girls felt obliged to eat their final meal in the dining room with Lydia's father that evening. He was not good company but Lydia could tell that he appreciated the kindness. Her father had aged terribly over the past week due to a combination of stress and his wound. He appeared far frailer than she would have thought possible and the confident, blusterous man she was used to had been replaced by a nervous, introspective wreck of a human being. His skin had lost its pale clammy appearance thanks to Master Berant's healing but her father's eyes remained sunken and red with dark shadows beneath.

Elaine hardly knew Lydia's father but even she felt a stirring of pity for him. It was far clearer to her than Lydia (who was quite understandably denying the facts) that Thomas was facing utter ruin. It was unlikely that Lydia's fortunes would fall as low as Elaine's own but nonetheless Lydia's standing and prospects on the island were bound to suffer. Though she cared little for such things herself, Elaine was concerned for her friend's future. It would be painful to see Lydia suffer social slights and become a pariah as a result of something utterly removed from her control. Given that such an outcome seemed inevitable, all Elaine could do was privately resolve to stand fast by her cousin and offer what comfort she could.

The awkward meal drew to a close eventually with a few clumsy words from Lydia's father about taking care of themselves. What he was trying to say was that he'd miss having them around but it didn't come out that way. Having failed miserably to say what he wanted, Thomas allowed the girls to escape his poor company and go up to their rooms.

He remained alone in the dining room as the candles burned slowly down. His thoughts turned to fatherhood and the fact that Lydia was no longer a child but a young lady. If there was some small comfort from the situation it was that his daughter was old enough, and sufficiently strong willed, to ride out the troubled times ahead of her. Though he could scarcely claim credit he was proud of her nonetheless.

A sharp knocking at the front door broke into his thoughts and a few seconds later, Captain Skelder was ushered into the room. Thomas sprang to his feet, a fierce fire burning suddenly in his eyes and colour returning to his cheeks.

"Ah, Skelder! There is much to discuss and very little time." There was still a little fight left in him, Thomas knew, and he still had much to play for.

From their vantage point in Elaine's room, the two girls watched Thomas's elaborate deception. Two improbably awkward and bulky "girls" climbed into the carriage which rattled off at a brisk trot with an inadequate escort of three men. Five minutes later, a squad of ten of Skelder's best men rode out after it.

"The bait and the trap," Elaine observed. "Neat. Do you think it will work?"

"Maybe," Lydia shrugged nervously. "If it does, that means someone really was out there waiting to get us!"

"Well, we won't be there will we?" Elaine dismissed the thought. "We'll be enjoying a fine night out on the Cathe. Talking of which, there go our belongings. Time we made a move, Lydia. Let's leave all this behind us, shall we? It's all over now."

"Yes, all over," Lydia repeated, wondering just how much of her life "all" included.

The precautions taken to smuggle the girls out unnoticed were almost comical had not Thomas been in such a state of agitation that his anxiety passed to the girls too. Heavily cloaked, they were smuggled through the kitchen and took a lengthy route to the steps leading down to the boathouse. It was at the top of these that Thomas said his farewells, kissing Elaine's hand and giving his daughter a brief, rough hug. Finally, he pressed an envelope into Lydia's hand.

"Your mother wanted you to have this, my dear," he said. "Open it later. Now, run along girls! You must be well away from here by dawn."

"Goodbye father!" Lydia replied. "I'll write soon. Take care of yourself."

"I will, Child. Don't you worry about me!" He watched the pair run lightly down to the boathouse, unable to see the tears on Lydia's cheeks. He had intended to return to the house immediately to await Skelder's return but now that it came to it, Skelder could be damned. He pulled his cloak tighter about himself and waited.

There was little preparation needed inside the boathouse. Elaine had made everything ready and their belongings were already stowed aboard. Badly stowed, Elaine noticed with a frown. How anyone on the island could be as ignorant of the sea as the Wescliffe household was beyond her. There was no time to worry about that now however.

"Jump aboard," Elaine ordered her cousin with an encouraging grin. "Take the helm. We won't be mooring this time, so head for the mouth of the cov as soon as she'll answer the tiller. I'll do the rest."

"Aye Cap'n." Despite all the other emotions, Lydia couldn't help but feel excited by the prospect of the night's sail ahead of her. She hastily wiped her face with the back of her hand and took her place. It was impossible not to pick up some of her friend's enthusiasm. Elaine heaved on the counter weight hanging at the front of the boathouse. The oiled hinges made no sound as the doors swung open. Silver moonlight poured softly into the building as Elaine moved along the gantry and down the stairs. She was breathing deeply, calming herself. Nerves or excitement could make her clumsy she knew. This was no time for a silly mistake.

Looking down from her perch, Lydia saw Elaine take the heavy hammer down from its hook and test the balance. Aiming carefully, she swung it and as before struck the pin squarely, releasing the windlass mechanism.

On the last occasion, SKYLARK had been beached for a number of years and so had moved reluctantly from her resting place. Not so tonight. With less than two weeks since the last launch, the grooves in the stone floor were free of moss and other debris. Also, the oiled mechanism of the windlass offered much less resistance. The boat began to move immediately, pulling chain behind it in a glittering stream. Elaine was quick. She was halfway up the rickety steps before the handle of the hammer struck the floor but Lydia's face was moving away from her by the time she gained the gantry.

With no time to think, Elaine put on her best burst of speed and vaulted the end rail recklessly, hurling herself at the SKYLARK's stern. Her hands found the stern rail but the rest of her missed completely and so when SKYLARK emerged from the boathouse it was with a small figure hanging from the back of it.

The speed was exhilarating. Elaine could feel the hull trembling next to her as it accelerated down the ramp. Then there was a rapid deceleration as the bows met the water and raised a veil of spray around the boat. The problem occurred as the bows recovered and rose back out of the sea. By a simple process of cause and effect, this drove the stern downwards ducking Elaine up to her chest in icy water. She barely had time to gasp in shock before a grinning Lydia hauled her into the cockpit.

"Welcome aboard, Cap'n! Bit nippy for a swim, don't you think?"

"You..." Elaine left the witty retort unsaid. She hurried forward to raise the mast and set the sails, squelching as she went and leaving a glistening wet trail in her wake.

From his vantage, Thomas D'Shan had not seen the mishap on the slipway, but he did see the yacht slide silently into the centre of the cov where, after a brief delay, she began to spread silver sails. The sails caught the wind immediately and SKYLARK heeled and turned, gathering speed and heading out to sea. He watched until the small speck disappeared into the haze outside the mouth of the cov's entrance. A single tear was hastily brushed away before his face became composed and set in a stern expression. Thomas D'Shan turned on his heel and strode purposefully back to the house. The girls were out of his care now. The next priority was to see to his own affairs.

Once clear of the coast, Elaine ducked below the gunwale and changed into some dry clothes. By the time she raised her head again SKYLARK was bounding down the Cathe with the wind dead aft. There was a much greater swell tonight than on their previous trip. This and the fact that the wind was not on SKYLARK's best point of sailing would mean that they were not going to make quite such good time. Elaine was not worried by this. The nearest ships to them were much further out in the Cathe and outrunning any of them, should that prove necessary, would be an easy matter.

"You all right there?" she asked Lydia.

"Never better!" Lydia's hand was confident on the tiller. She had thrown back her hood and Elaine could see her friend's cheeks aglow with the chill. Her whole being was alive with excitement; the heavy burden of worry and fear having been left behind. Not wanting to spoil the moment for her friend, Elaine busied herself about the ropes and allowed Lydia to enjoy herself.

Lights were readied but not lit. In the slight haze caused by spray whipping off the white capped waves, SKYLARK would be all but invisible from both the shore and any of the other vessels the girls could see in the distance. That suited their purposes and although technically they should have been showing lights, Elaine decided against it. They were well out of the main shipping routes and no vessel was near.

"Would you like a bun?" Elaine offered when she eventually joined Lydia in the cockpit.

"Yes please! Hungry work this running away," Lydia chuckled. "I can't believe father allowed us to take the boat! Will we get many chances to sail her do you think?" Elaine shook her head, her mouth full of bun.

"Probably not," she said a moment later. "CovTol is very tricky to get out of. The wind has to be just right otherwise you get pulled onto the rocks. Easy enough to get in – usually. This wind's all very well now but we won't be able to take her in until it changes. Still, there's no sense worrying about that just yet. That's a good few hours away." Elaine didn't add that the swell, lively enough out here, would be treacherous indeed on their approach to CovTol's narrow rock-guarded entrance. If any boat could do it, this one could she reasoned.

SKYLARK certainly seemed at home on the Cathe. Although bucking quite wildly on occasion, she was shipping very little water. This didn't prevent plenty of salt spray finding its way aft, wetting the girls' faces and getting into their mouths. The experience was altogether different to their day trip. Their surroundings were limited by darkness and sea haze. Waves appeared as dark masses, capped with white that fluoresced in the moonlight. The set of the swell meant that the bow reared occasionally, seeming to point skywards towards the distant stars before plunging towards the dark mass of the sea. At the point where it seemed that it should engulf them, the mass dissolved to spray and flew icily into their grinning faces.

"Look!" Lydia started up in alarm, her arm thrown forward. "I saw something in the water, just off the bow. Shall I turn?"

"Steady!" Elaine snapped the order. Any sudden turn risked broaching SKYLARK in the heavy seas which would be very bad indeed. "Where away?"

"Port bow." Lydia had forgotten the first rule in her agitation. Always give a bearing. Both girls strained their eyes to catch the object again. After a moment they saw it together; a sleek silver shape broke through the side of a wave and dived headlong into the next snatching a breath as it did so.

"Dolphin!" Elaine sighed with relief. "Just keeping an eye on us!"

"Will we hurt it?" Lydia was concerned as the dolphin was very close aboard.

"Not us!" Elaine smiled as the shape leaped clear again. She reached down into the bottom of the cockpit to where a small bucket of fish scraps was stored. She tossed a small handful overboard. "Fair winds and safe return," Elaine said softly, tapping the hull twice.

"Sorry?" Lydia hadn't quite caught the words.

"A sailor's charm," Elaine explained slightly embarrassed. "You

always offer dolphins food. It's supposed to bring good luck."

"I never object to some of that," Lydia agreed turning her attention back to steering. "Are you sure you don't want a turn?"

"You're fine." Elaine leaned over the side, watching the smooth

movements of the dolphin until it moved ahead and out of sight.

SKYLARK rounded the Sor-most point of Fain-Arn as the first pink light of dawn tinged the wispy clouds on the horizon. This brought the girls to some of the most dangerous waters in the whole kingdom of Thirnmar. To starboard they could make out the coastline of Elledran, the largest of Fain-Arn's sister islands along the Cathe.

"We'll need to have our wits about us now," Elaine told Lydia, raising her voice slightly over the sound of the sea. "Up until now, we've only had the Cathe to deal with. The swell and currents are mostly governed by Thirnmar on one side and Fain-Arn and Ror on the other. This is where it gets tricky. You see the promontory over there on Elledran?" Lydia nodded.

"I see it. The one with a tower?"

"That's it. It marks the narrowest point of Carras Sound which runs from here all the way up to Carran Thum. The currents from along there are channelled to this point where they meet those from the Cathe. They can change very quickly – which is why they built TolSor and the tower over on Elledran. Many a ship has been driven ashore along here." Lydia's face took on an expression of alarm, but Elaine patted her arm reassuringly. "Don't worry, I know what I'm doing!" Elaine took the tiller from Lydia. She had sailed these waters since the age of seven. As often happens, the wind shifted a few points as the light of dawn strengthened but the wind was too eager. They were not yet in position to take advantage of it and so the girls found themselves tacking into the wind with the strong swell of the Cathe on their beam and the conflicting but as yet weaker swell of Carras Sound meeting the bows.

"We're going to have to beat into this for a while!" Elaine had to shout to make herself heard over the crashing seas about their small craft. It was louder now with spray bursting explosively over the boat.

Lydia didn't reply. The heavy motion was awakening some unpleasant feelings within her and she was gulping down fresh air to try to stem the nausea. She fought it hard, but the violent corkscrew pitch SKYLARK adopted at the start of their second tack was too much for her and Lydia shared her misery with the sea as they scudded back and forth under the strengthening light.

The first proper glimpse of the sun found the girls finally in position to attempt the entrance to CovTol. Lydia's sickness had, by now, run its course and although very pale she was feeling much better.

"I'm going to start our run in now," Elaine said. Her face was set in an expression of grim concentration. This was perhaps the greatest test of her skills to date. Aside from the challenge of making the entrance, the conditions were by no means benign and she was drawing on every last bit of her experience to navigate SKYLARK safely.

This involved several skills, some of which she was hardly aware she possessed. All at once she had to be part of the boat, aware of the strain on the hull, mast, sails and rigging. She had, too, to be part of the sea, reading the passage of the waves to pick the best way through the confused swell. She had to read the wind, anticipating short sudden gusts whose cunning and malice she knew all too well could cause a boat to capsize.

Finally, and hardest of all, Elaine had to anticipate the effect of the currents moving them back towards the Cathe. She had to ensure that they would arrive at the mouth of CovTol, rather than onto the rocks either side of the entrance. Lydia was just experienced enough to know how difficult this landfall was going to be. She would certainly have never attempted such a thing by herself. She remained quietly out of the way as Elaine leaned out to starboard, into the wind, to get the best view ahead as she made the difficult judgement.

As the cliffs grew nearer, Elaine's heart skipped with the realisation that she had got it right. If anything, she had been overcautious, but that was easily corrected. Had she misjudged it the other way, by drifting too close to the rocks on the far side of the cov, there would have been no saving them.

Knowing that the water was deepest on their side of the cov, Elaine took them in as close as she dared, much to Lydia's discomfort. Spray from the wicked rocks splashed their faces as they swept by. In an instant, everything changed. The waters were now sheltered and calm. The sails fell slack but SKYLARK was no lubberly fishing vessel and had sufficient way on her to glide gently on to the centre of the small cov. Her deep racing keel made Elaine unwilling to attempt the stone jetty, however. On her command, Lydia dropped the anchor over the bow whilst they were still in relatively deep water.

The sails came down next and had to be securely stowed. Elaine absolutely refused to consider going ashore until everything aboard SKYLARK was as it should be. The girls spent a good hour in the strengthening sun which provided only feeble warmth in answer to the bitter wind. When at last all was ready, Lydia spotted a problem.

"Elaine, how do we get ashore?" A small gig was visible on the shale beach but it was pulled up well above the high tide mark and no-one had come down from TolSor, whose tower was just visible, to greet them.

"How do you think?" Elaine grinned wildly. She had slipped back into her wet clothes from the previous night. Lydia's expression was priceless.

"You must be joking!"

"It's alright, I'll come back for you in the gig. We'll need it for our trunks anyway. Back in a tick." With that, Elaine stepped onto the gunwale and dived gracefully into the sea with hardly a splash.

The sea was wickedly cold and took her breath away but Elaine often swam in the sea, even in winter, and so she was ready for it. From experience she knew the best way to deal with it was to swim briskly, which she did. Her dive was deep and she swam hard for the shore underwater. Lydia was much relieved to see the dark mop of hair break the surface a short distance from the jetty. Elaine shunned the stone steps and swam on until her feet found the steeply shelving beach.

The wind lanced through her wet clothes like a thousand pins pricking her skin as she ran up the beach. The effort of dragging the heavy gig back down to the water by herself generated a fair bit of warmth as did the row back out to SKYLARK. Lydia immediately passed a towel to her friend and fussed until she had changed back into a dry shirt and warm jumper. She then helped Elaine lower their things into the gig before following them down herself.

As they rowed ashore Lydia looked about her, taking in the details of their surroundings in the fresh morning light. In geographical terms, CovTol was very similar to Wescliffe's own cov. The difference lay in orientation (Sor, not Wes) and the set of tide and currents at the entrance. As at Wescliffe, the cov was enclosed on two sides by sheer rock and on the third by a steeply shelving shale beach. A narrow track ran from the beach to the high ground where TolSor had been built to warn shipping to stay clear. Since the end of the dark period in the Kingdom's history known as the Age of Strife, when wreckers had plied their gruesome trade on all of the islands, the showing of a light out to sea meant only one thing: Keep Away.

The keel of the gig scrunched against the shale and broke into Lydia's thoughts. Elaine hopped over the side and ran up the beach with the bow rope to secure the boat. Lydia's exit was rather more reluctant. The cold water caused her trousers to cling to her legs and made her gasp. She grabbed hold of a rope with Elaine and between them they hauled the gig a short way up the beach. Anything more than that would have to be accomplished without the heavy trunks being aboard. Elaine assessed the situation quickly and was satisfied.

"How about breakfast?" she asked.

"That sounds very good to me," Lydia replied sincerely.

Chapter Eight - TolSor

For Elaine, the ascent up the steep path was a return to an environment which was both familiar and comforting. For Lydia, it was an ascent into an entirely new world. She approached the experience with the same mixture of excitement and nervous anticipation as Elaine had her own arrival at Wescliffe.

TolSor was a square tower, tall and slender, constructed of large granite blocks. At its base, facing the sea, a solid door was set into a slight recess in the wall. Built at a time when the wreckers had not been fully suppressed, TolSor had been designed with defensibility in mind. In many ways it resembled a small castle, in that the only windows were narrow slits and the door looked as though it had been built to withstand siege weaponry. A glass gazebo-like structure on the roof betrayed the tower's true purpose. Within the glass enclosure was the lamp that it was the keeper's duty to maintain and light.

Originally the tower keeper and his family would have led a cramped existence within the tower itself. Though solid, the tower was not large in its proportions and offered only meagre accommodation space within it. In more peaceful times the accommodation had been improved by constructing a single storey longhouse next to the tower and it was this that Elaine called home.

Lydia's first impression of the exterior was that it was very small. The eaves barely cleared the top of the small windows and the entire length of the house represented the distance from Wescliffe's front door to the end of the dining room (the room immediately next to the front door!). It appeared welcoming enough as Elaine's mother was a house-proud woman when the baby permitted. The stone walls had been recently whitewashed and the narrow glass panes gleamed in the sun. Smudges of wood smoke were sporadically snatched from the chimney indicating the presence of warmth within.

Elaine's experienced eyes caught a number of causes for concern that her cousin missed. Immediately in front of the house was the vegetable garden. This was her father's domain and had clearly been neglected of late. There were a number of other smaller things she spotted: a broken gutter, the odd tile that had slipped. All of these told her that her father must be quite ill. Nothing short of being bedridden would keep him from quickly tending to such jobs.

The girls went around the end of the house and entered through the back door. Much to Lydia's surprise, this opened directly into the kitchen. Hallways - useful for keeping draughts at bay - were a luxury which belonged to larger houses. Despite this, TolSor's kitchen welcomed them with warmth and the sight of a steaming kettle on the range. Elaine hastily closed the door behind them and kicked off her boots which joined a pile in the corner next to the door.

"Welcome to TolSor," she grinned. "Tea?"

"Yes please!" Lydia removed her own boots and placed them neatly next to the pile without noticing Elaine's smile.

"Grab a couple of mugs could you?" Elaine pointed to a row of china mugs hanging from hooks on a beam above the table.

"Where on earth did you get these?" Lydia exclaimed, examining the faded but still visible royal coat of arms.

"They come with the tower," Elaine explained, pouring the scalding water expertly into the mugs with a towel wrapped round the handle of the kettle to protect her hands. "The tea's in the blue tin on that shelf," she added.

Lydia had never seen tea made directly in a drinking mug before. Elaine put a pinch of tea into a kind of mesh ball which was dropped into the mug. A minute later, after a brisk stir, she fished it out and repeated the process with the other mug. She had just finished when her mother came in, wiping her hands on her apron.

"There you are, Elaine!" and with a nod at the brimming mugs, "I'd love one!" Elaine laughed.

"Extra mug, Lydia!"

"Thank you, dears." After giving her daughter a rough but warm hug, Sasha Sheldon sank wearily into the bow chair at the head of the table. "Excuse me, Lydia, where are my manners? Welcome to TolSor. I trust your journey was pleasant?"

"Exciting, I'd say Aunt Sasha," Lydia replied. "We came by boat. Are you sure it's alright my staying here? I don't want to put you to any trouble."

"Of course it's alright!" Elaine's mother exclaimed. "You're family. Besides, there's so much to do. I'm sure Elaine will be grateful for an extra pair of hands."

"How is father?" Elaine asked anxiously. "Can I see him?"

"He's sleeping at present. He's quite ill, dear, you know how he gets. David's asleep too; at last. I expect they'll wake each other presently. Now girls, what's this I hear about trouble at Wescliffe? Some of the stories I've been hearing are so wild they can't possibly be true!"

TolSor received deliveries of food and general supplies for the tower every week from Perth Cathe. The cart driver, by virtue of his rounds, was able to convey the important "news" of the island to all of his customers. Not even the King's Post on the main island could convey news over distance more efficiently than Fain-Arn's gossip network. It was said that news, particularly bad news, travelled faster than the tide from one end of the island to the other.

Elaine examined her mother closely as Lydia gave a heavily edited account of the past two weeks. For some reason a faint alarm bell was sounding. Her mother looked tired, certainly, but there was something else there too. Was there a slight nervousness perhaps? Reserve? Or something else? Elaine dismissed the thought as it formed. Most likely her mother had mixed feelings about having her wealthy niece coming to stay but was doing her best to hide the fact.

"Well, perhaps you're better off out of the way here for a while. I trust your father will recover soon," Sasha said kindly when Lydia's account had finished. Then to Elaine: "Now love, I've some baking to do before David wakes up. There's some of yesterday's bread in the larder with some jam for your breakfast. Perhaps afterwards you had better get your trunks brought up to the house and stowed. Then you can show Lydia around. Try not to wake the men though!"

After a meagre but very welcome breakfast, the girls managed to get the heavy trunks up the steep path and stowed under the beds in Elaine's tiny room. Though small, cold and draughty with its cracked window pane and bare whitewashed walls, it was a strangely cosy and welcoming little room. A china basin rested on a wash stand at the foot of Elaine's bed. A small writing desk, on which stood a vase containing fresh cut flowers, faced out of the window so that the writer might enjoy both light and air. A threadbare rug covered much of the space between the two beds but the real feature of the room was the bedding. Sasha Sheldon disliked tapestry as much as her daughter but took a real delight in crochet. The beds were well covered with brightly coloured crochet wool blankets over plain linen sheets. The colours lent illusionary warmth to the room in the autumn sunlight.

Lydia felt awkward, sensing her cousin's conflicting feelings. On one hand, Elaine was aware that her home was very plain and humble. It troubled her slightly that Lydia had probably not realised quite how different their two worlds were. On the other hand, she was proud of her home and particularly her room which was very much her own space. With a degree of tact not inherited from either parent, Lydia complimented without being patronising and in a short while the awkwardness passed. In a curious way, Lydia realised she could be more "herself" here than ever she could at Wescliffe or Harton.

"Can I see the lamp?" she asked eventually when she had seen the stables and piggery and "stolen" a freshly baked bun from the kitchen for them both.

"I expect so," Elaine said. "I'll have to check. It's all changed up there, mother says, since this new contraption went in. I'm not sure if it's safe." At that moment there came a shrill and indignant howl from the main bedroom as David awoke to a wet nappy and gnawing hunger.

"Girls!" Elaine's mother summoned them to the kitchen. "What's it to be, nursing or washing up?"

"Nursing!" The two girls replied at once.

"I'll fetch him then," Sasha said with a smile.

While she washed and tidied away the baking debris, Elaine's mother had a wonderful time watching out of the corner of her eye as the two girls battled with changing the baby and feeding him his bottle. The latter proved easy enough but the former was a considerable challenge. The end result was a baby swathed from the armpits down in multiple layers of towelling tied off with a selection of sturdy nautical knots. The girls were very pleased with themselves and Sasha chose not to comment on their efforts.

75

"Oh, Elaine, your father wants to see you. Don't stay too long though, he tires easily." Elaine handed the gurgling and satisfied baby over to Lydia and made her way next door. She opened the door gently and slipped into her parents' room.

The curtains were drawn but the material was thin and a soft pale light filtered through. Immediately inside the door was the swing crib where David slept. Her father was propped up in bed surrounded by extra pillows and the bolster. Even in the half-light, Elaine could see he was pale and feverish. His eyes appeared to have shrunk into their sockets and his breathing was laboured and noisy. Elaine was horrified but hastily mastered the feeling lest her face betray it. Instead she smiled gently and clasped her father's hand, perching herself carefully on the edge of the bed. Her hand received a gentle squeeze and her father's eyes opened.

"Hullo our kid," he whispered. "Back alright then?"

"Yes thank you. How are you feeling?"

"Not at my best, love, but I'll mend. Don't you fret. Did Lydia come with you?"

"Yes. There's been a bit of bother at Wescliffe." Her father averted his face and coughed harshly into a handkerchief.

"Nice company for you at any rate," he said eventually. "Listen, love. I'm no damned good to man nor beast at present. Your mother's got enough on with the young'un. I need you to look after this place for a while, 'till I'm up again."

"Of course! Lydia will help too."

"I'm sure," her father said dryly.

"No, she will," Elaine insisted. "She's a lot like me really, 'cept she's had a different life. She's not lazy though. That's not a family trait." Dan smiled grimly, wincing with pain as he shifted slightly.

"Sorry, dear. I shouldn't leap to judgements. Now, about the tower..."

Elaine stayed no more than a quarter of an hour at her father's bedside. During that time, she learned about the new mechanisms installed to improve the working of the lamp and what her father would need her and Lydia to do each day. When she returned to the kitchen, Elaine found David asleep in her mother's arms and Lydia finishing the last of the washing up. Only the look of concentration on her cousin's face betrayed the fact that she had very little experience of this type of work. Elaine helped Lydia by wiping off the last of the dishes before offering to take her up the tower.

"Not a pleasure trip, I'm afraid," Elaine warned. "There are a few jobs that need doing."

"Fine." Lydia waited impatiently as Elaine, having removed a huge key from a nail in the hallway, struggled with the lock on the door connecting the house to the tower. This inner door was every bit as formidable as the main door to the tower but Elaine beat it eventually. The two girls entered the oldest part of TolSor.

Lydia found that her eyes needed time to grow used to the dim light which shafted in through three narrow slits high up on two of the walls. Eventually she could make out the room about her. Next to the back wall, stretching out into the room, was a large oak table with a bench each side of it. In the opposite corner of the room to where they were standing was a large open stone fireplace. The space between the fireplace and the front wall was filled with a jumble of boxes and large earthenware jars. On their right, tucked away in the corner, was the entrance to a narrow spiral staircase. The wooden beams supporting the next floor were high up above their heads, easily some twenty feet above them. The whole place smelled of damp soot, presumably a problem with the ancient chimney.

"This is the working/dining area," Elaine explained. "Before the house was built, this would have been the kitchen, storage and living room."

"Not much in the way of comforts," Lydia observed, taking in the stone floor and bare walls. "Cosy enough, I suppose, with the fire lit."

"Claustrophobic though." Elaine shuddered. "I can't imagine being cooped up in here all day! Now we mostly use it for stores. Those jars are for the lamp oil. We'll see more of them later," she added ominously. "Next floor is the sleeping quarters. It's a bit nicer. Mother keeps it clean in case we need it."

A fair climb up the narrow stairs brought them to a doorway onto the next level of the tower.

"This isn't too bad!" Lydia exclaimed once she was in the room. Like the floor below, this level had an open fireplace, although it was smaller. There were more slit windows admitting light and several rugs decorated the floor. One corner of the room was partitioned with wooden panelling and a curtain by way of a door. This contained bunk beds made up with the trademark crochet blankets. Between the partition and the fireplace was a double bed equally ready to accommodate sleepers. The room had a pleasant feel, as if it was ready to welcome guests at a moment's notice, though here too there was more than a hint of damp in the air.

"We sleep up here if the weather turns bad," Elaine explained. "Father needs to be handy for the lamp and sometimes I help out if it's really awful and mother needs a rest. We've been known to be in the tower for several nights at a time. That's usually in the spring time. The weather can be pretty awful then, you know that!"

"Yes, Wescliffe's pretty exposed," Lydia agreed.

"Want to see the interesting bit?" Elaine asked.

"The lamp?"

"Not quite, one more floor to go first. Come on!"

The next climb brought them to a large, plain, functional chamber beneath the roof of the tower. Lydia gaped in wonder at the spider's web of wires and chains leading from windlasses through various blocks and hoops to a clockwork mechanism suspended in the centre of the ceiling. When her eyes travelled down from this, she noticed a large box in the centre of the room. From the front of the box protruded a giant cone, like a speaking trumpet, which stretched through the front wall to the outside.

"Foghorn," Elaine explained. "Look." Behind the box was a platform on which to stand. From the back of the box a brass handle emerged. "You turn that, pretty fast, and a big fan starts up inside the box." Elaine gestured at the contraption. "Next thing you know it's humming away. The horn carries the sound outside although it's pretty loud in here too! We were told they heard it on Elledran once; the wind was from the Nor that day which is pretty rare. The worst storms are Sor-Westers. Even then it still carries a fair way. In fog or bad weather we have to sound it every four minutes for thirty seconds twice, with a thirty second break. That's half as often as the lamp flashes you see. Hard work!"

"I can imagine," Lydia agreed trying to hide her desire to try the thing out.

"I can't rightly tell you what all that does!" Elaine pointed at the mechanism on the ceiling. "It's all new. All I do know is that it operates on weights, like a clock. There are four big weights and they need winding up each day. Guess what?"

"That's another of our little jobs?" Lydia hazarded.

"Hah!" We'll make a tower keeper of you yet," Elaine chuckled. "Best get it over with."

The next forty minutes were borrowed from purgatory as far as Lydia was concerned. The windlasses were designed to be operated by the likes of Elaine's father who was a broad-shouldered man accustomed to heavy work. Elaine, too, was used to exertion but lacked the weight and reach to make the windlass turn with any speed. Lydia was hopelessly ill-equipped to cope but did her share nonetheless, even though the effort half killed her. Each weight required precisely one hundred and twenty-five turns to raise it to the roof again. The girls took it in shifts of fifty turns. Only when the nightmare was over did they venture up the last part of the stairs to the roof.

There, Lydia's weariness, aching arms and shoulders were forgotten as she took in the breath-taking view. But for a few white scudding clouds the sky was clear and she could see for miles. On one side was the distant coast of Elledran beyond which rose the faint peaks of that island's mountains. From the next side of the tower Elaine pointed out the row of abandoned beacon towers which stretched in an arc across the peninsula towards Perth Cathe. The port was hidden from their view by high ground, but beyond the towers the Cathe sparkled in the sun, flashing white in a line where it met the distant coast of Thirnmar.

"You can't see much of Fain-Arn from here," Elaine said eventually, having given Lydia time to take in the view. "Corech Forn is that ridge of trees on the skyline over there. If we come up again after dark, you'll be able to see TolEste if it stays this clear. They show a red light every two minutes for one minute; they've had a clockwork thing put in as well. The beacon on Elledran hasn't, as far as I know. They just show a constant light the same as we used to."

"You must miss this when, you know, you're stuck at school," Lydia said looking at her cousin who seemed suddenly so full of life despite the day's hard work on top of a night's sailing. The brisk wind caught her dark hair, throwing it out behind her. Elaine's cheeks were colouring in the cold wind and her eyes seemed to catch the glittering light of the sea.

"I do," Elaine admitted. "It's nice to come back to though; makes you appreciate it a bit more I suppose." They inspected the lantern next in its small glass room. There was little space inside now that the mirrors and revolving screens had been installed to make the lamp "flash". Elaine showed Lydia how to fill the lamp and trim the wick ready for lighting. She noticed that two of the three oil jars were empty but decided to put that job off until tomorrow. Each jar contained enough oil for four night's burning, under normal conditions, and so they still had some in hand.

They spent a full hour on the roof before going down. When dusk fell at about six o'clock, Lydia was allowed to light the lamp. They then hastily scrambled downstairs to set the clockwork mechanism in gear. Lydia tried not to think about those giant weights slowly sinking ready to be hoisted again tomorrow – her hands were blistered and raw from winding though she had not complained.

Elaine's mother insisted that they went to bed early and both girls were happy to oblige. Though nowhere near as soft as the bed she was used to, even at school, Lydia's bed seemed like a haven of warmth and comfort that night.

Chapter Nine - Forngarth

TolSor days start early and despite not really being a "morning person", Lydia woke at the same time as Elaine in the first light of early dawn. David had kept Elaine's mother awake for much of the night and so, while Lydia washed in the cold water of the basin, Elaine cleared the ash from the range and lit the fire.

The girls swapped over once Lydia had finished. By the time Elaine had washed and dressed the kettle was steaming near to the boil and a plate of sliced and buttered bread was on the table. Lydia had packed a few supplies from Wescliffe's kitchen, including oats, and while the girls ate bread and drank scalding tea to warm themselves, a pot of porridge was set on the range for "late breakfast". They would eat this once their jobs in the tower were complete.

After dowsing the lamp and refilling the reservoir, the girl's next job was to wind the weights back up. If anything, it was harder for Lydia than the first time because she was still aching from yesterday. Stubbornly, she refused to do less than her share and Elaine assured her that she'd get used to it in a day or so. This encouragement was offered as much for her own benefit as Lydia's since Elaine also found the winding quite strenuous.

"We'd better change the oil jars over today," Elaine added when the two girls had caught their breath. "The jars only last about three nights each and we've used most of the last jar. Father likes to keep a good supply on hand in case the weather turns nasty. More lifting and winding, I'm afraid, although I'll do most of it. I'll need you downstairs with the guide rope."

"We can't get them up the stairs, surely?" Lydia queried nervously.

"Of course not!" Elaine chuckled. "There are trap doors on each floor and the roof. We just raise and lower them using the crane next to the lamp room. Actually, it's an old davit off a wrecked barque but it does the job. Father rigged a couple of extra blocks to make it easy enough for me to use."

The girls opened the three trap doors allowing daylight to pour deep into the tower from the roof. Elaine quickly made the crane ready and lowered a sturdy rope down to the store room far below where Lydia was waiting. Although the jars were stored more or less below the trap doors, the first required shifting slightly to get it into position. It was incredibly heavy and Lydia was puffing with exhaustion by the time it began its slow ascent to the roof. Lydia could only guess at the effort required by Elaine to move it into the lamp room. In seemingly no time at all an empty jar sailed majestically down. The entire process was repeated twice more before the girls joined Sasha and David for "late breakfast" which was, by that time, most welcome!

At much the same time as the girls were settling down to their porridge, Groth found himself in yet another smart waiting room. Unlike Thomas D'Shan's at Wescliffe, Groth entered this waiting room only by invitation and with some trepidation. He was eventually ushered through to the inner office by a nervous, pale, bean-pole man in a black clerk's coat. Whatever scorn he might have felt for this excuse-of-a-man, he kept to himself. It did not do to insult even the lowliest of his patron's employees.

"Groth! Kind of you to come." Groth's patron sat in a magnificent leather chair behind a polished and uncluttered desk. He was a large man in both height and weight. His clothes were well tailored and of the highest quality. A silver watch chain adorned his waistcoat. Mr Jewkes removed his glasses and fixed Groth with a stern gaze. "I seem to be owed some money," he observed. "I trust there is not a problem?"

"Nothing long-term, I assure you," Groth replied smoothly. "Only a very small amount of the shipment was lost with the boat."

"Then why the delay? I do not like delay, Mr Groth, particularly in relation to payment. The Revenue Officer does not have the goods. You do not have them. If you did you'd be at the bottom of the Cathe by now." Jewkes' voice was emotionless. Unlike Thomas D'Shan, who had fallen prey to Groth, Mr Jewkes was a different class of man and both knew it. Jewkes owned three large wool mills – the principle industry and source of low income employment on the island. He had innumerable business interests of a legitimate nature and several very illegitimate ones. His calling card was extreme violence, or sudden death, delivered at the hand of thugs from Thirnmar who were far rougher than the contacts Groth dealt with. Jewkes was untouchable. Groth was a very lowly worm by comparison.

"I will find the shipment, sir. I have people looking in all the likely places. It will be recovered, and there will be a charge to those hiding it for late delivery."

"Perhaps if you put less effort into settling your own petty grudge against D'Shan you might be more successful?" Jewkes suggested mildly. Groth concealed his anger with difficulty.

"D'Shan is largely responsible for getting us into this mess, Sir. I am merely looking to insure myself, and therefore you, against any loss."

"So your frantic search for D'Shan's daughter is professional, not personal?" Jewkes raised a sceptical eyebrow. "My sources tell me the girls made a fool of you."

"Rubbish!" Groth began strongly before moderating his tone hastily. "Daren Berant got involved and the girls escaped with him. He cannot be everywhere, however. The girls must return to school shortly."

"I sincerely hope I won't have to wait that long for my money!" Jewkes' voice became cold and low. "Groth, find the shipment OR find the girls, but do it fast! I have my own reputation as a man of business to consider. I will have my money in the next four days. If I do not, your usefulness will cease and you would do well to run very far away indeed. That is all. You know your way out I believe?"

Groth made his way hastily from the mill and set out on the road to Perth Cathe. It was there that his contacts were most numerous and reliable. He would make some enquiries about the shipment but, in truth, he was not hopeful on that score. His main determination was to lay his hands on Lydia and her friend. That would ensure money from Thomas D'Shan and allow him to settle a score in the process. Elaine's fate, he decided, would be particularly nasty.

At TolSor, as the last of the "late breakfast" dishes were being washed, there came a loud knock on the front door. Sasha went to open it, hastily wiping her hands on her apron. She was gone quite a long time and the girls could hear voices talking and laughing. Finally, Elaine's mother returned to the kitchen bringing a tall and smartly dressed man in tow.

"Girls, this is Mr Brown. He's the coachman at Forngarth. You have been invited to afternoon tea and to attend the Harvest Home supper. Mr Brown will drive you there and back but you must be quick! Wash yourselves again; you're covered in filth from the tower and change into something presentable! No Elaine, use the pump. I'll not have it said I can't keep my daughter clean! I'll set out your best dress in a moment. Tea, Mr Brown?"

If a quick wash using the cold water in the basin was a bracing experience, words are hardly adequate to describe the sensation of being dowsed under a pump gushing water straight from a well in late autumn. Elaine pumped energetically while Lydia stuck first her head (a shrill scream) and then the rest of her under the icy water. The importance of the occasion required the use of TolSor's only bar of soap; an ancient white mass which lathered only reluctantly and seemed to work mainly by the process of removing dirt and skin alike rather than any inherent cleaning power.

By the time Lydia had returned the favour by pumping icy water for her cousin, both girls felt as though they were glowing with cleanliness. After only half an hour they had passed inspection under Sasha's critical eye and were sitting inside the carriage belonging to Elaine's Grandmother, and Lydia's Great Aunt, Eleanor D'Shan of Math Forngath.

Elaine had repeated her choice of clothes from the meal at Wescliffe, seemingly so long ago now, complete with Lydia's additions. Lydia had selected what she called a "day dress" which was a pale lilac in colour with flounced embroidered sleeves. Her outfit was completed by a hat she had smuggled into her luggage without Elaine noticing - she had been under orders not to pack anything "unnecessary".

"You've done it again," Elaine remarked a little glumly. "You look great, Lydia." Her cousin didn't reply at first but stared blankly out of the window as the coach jolted along the uneven track at a fair pace.

"Might as well make the most of it while I can," she replied eventually. "I think Father's going to lose his job. Who knows what will happen then? I'm going to be the daughter of a disgraced man. Chances are I'll have to wear my pretty clothes, attract some rich man to marry quickly before word gets out, and move off the island."

"No, Lydia!" Elaine was horrified both by the idea and the despair in her friend's voice.

"I can't see much else awaits me." Lydia sighed then made an effort to appear cheerful. "But let's not talk about it today please! Anyway, how is it we're both being invited to tea when I'm supposed to be hiding in secret?" Elaine smiled in turn.

"Secrets aren't something Grandma has much time for! There's not much goes on she doesn't get to hear of, though how is a mystery to me."

"Oh." Lydia shifted in her seat. The dress was not comfortable to wear in a confined space. "I've never been to Forngarth, although I've heard quite a bit about it. What's Great Aunt Eleanor like?"

"Stern, old-fashioned but very nice. I think the headstrong part of my family comes from her! She and Mother are very much alike you know. When Mother fell in love with my father, Grandma stood up for them and got them installed in TolSor."

"She's not from Fain-Arn I understand," Lydia commented.

"Nor Thirnmar or any of the islands," Elaine answered. "She's from Wheldor. Her father was a merchant, part of a very wealthy family. Grandfather met her when his ship put into Whellan, that's a navy port on the Nor coast of the island. Grandma was working as a clerk in the warehouse and caught his eye. I expect she'll tell you about Wheldor if you ask. I love hearing her stories about the place. It sounds very different to here."

The girls chatted about nothing in particular as their coach bounced across the low meadow landscape. Finally, the coach began to climb an escarpment to the Downs on which Forngarth stood. The terrain here was similar to the scrubland near Wescliffe but it was less pitted and had fewer gorse bushes. Instead it was a rolling expanse of deep-green, well-populated with grazing animals. The road snaked through this wilderness, climbing slowly towards distant woodlands which appeared to embrace a large manor house. The girls had long since eaten the food, provided in the coach for their midday meal, by the time the scrunch of gravel beneath the wheels announced their destination.

Next to Math Calran, the governor's residence, Math Forngarth was the grandest house on the island. Rear Admiral Rupert D'Shan had been wealthy enough for a man of his social position. His marriage to the merchant's daughter from Wheldor, which had caused something of a stir at the time, had not harmed his fortune one bit and Forngarth was the result. Set in extensive grounds close to Corech Forn, Forngarth was an imposing three storey residence. It had been built in a more modern style than either Wescliffe or the older manor house which had been converted into the Harton School for Young Ladies.

Forngarth's windows were tall on the ground floor shrinking to small squares by the top floor which housed the remaining servants. This design created the appearance of height and grandeur. The front entrance comprised of a pair of double doors beneath a portico which extended out beyond three marble steps to allow guests to move under cover from their carriage into the house.

Since the death of Admiral D'Shan some five years earlier, his wife had taken over the running of the estate and lived alone with a much reduced household of servants. Nonetheless, it was evident from the immaculate grounds and the many crystal clear window panes that Eleanor D'Shan still lived in some style.

The girls were handed down from the coach by Mr Brown. They were just preparing to go up to the front doors when they noticed a second coach waiting by the house. Before they had time to wonder who it might belong to, both of the house doors were flung open and a heavily cloaked figure ran down the steps and hauled himself into the waiting coach.

Only briefly did they catch a glimpse of Tristan's scowling face before his own coachman urged the horses into a brisk trot. The look he cast the girls was venomous but in an instant he was gone. Lydia and Elaine exchanged a horrified glance before running up the stairs and entering the oak panelled hallway.

There was a timeless quality to Forngarth. Outside, the weather was cold and blustery. They had just seen a face they associated with fear and danger, yet in here everything was calm. A grand clock ticked loudly at the far end of the hall in the shadow of the wide staircase, which was carpeted in a deep red and swept grandly from a balcony above. Light flooded in through a glass dome in the roof high above them. Forngarth welcomed them as a safe port welcomes a ship in a storm. A high door, gilded with gold, opened on the left a short distance from the bottom of the stairs. Eleanor D'Shan came through to welcome her young guests.

She was dressed in a rich black dress well decorated with white lace - the only concession allowed to a widow - and a simple silver necklace with a sapphire pendant. Her hair was silver and worn long which was unusual for a lady of her years. Although she required an ebony cane, the old lady's back was straight; her eyes sharp and intelligent. Eleanor D'Shan's voice was strong and full of authority.

"Elaine, Lydia, welcome to Math Forngarth. I trust you are both well?"

"Very, thank you Grandma," Elaine replied with a slight bob.

"Quite well, Great Aunt, thank you." Lydia's curtsey was more practiced and earned her a slight nod from the elderly matriarch.

"Do come through dears. Tea is ready and I can't stand for too long in draughts. The doctor tells me that warmth and rest are important in one of my years, though what he knows about being my age I can't imagine! In my youth it was fresh air that was the thing but I do find that standing tires me." The grand old lady chattered on as she led the girls into the drawing room whose tall windows looked out onto sweeping lawns. The waters of Carras Sound glistened in the distance beyond the green sweep of the downs.

Tea was set out for them on a silver tea service with china plates bearing light sandwiches and cake. "Do the honours Elaine dear," the old lady ordered, easing herself gently into a high-backed chair and setting her cane next to it. Elaine hesitated.

"Grandma, wasn't that Tristan we just saw?"

"It was. Nasty young man he's turned into I must say!"

"Great Aunt, you must be careful!" Lydia exclaimed. "He's dangerous."

"Do hurry up with the tea dear," Eleanor rebuked Elaine mildly. She waited until the tea had been poured and they each had a plate with two bread triangles. "Dangerous?" she said eventually as if there had been no pause in the conversation at all. "Well, I suppose he is to some."

"No, really Grandma! Lydia's right," Elaine said, carefully swallowing her mouthful first. "He has the Gift."

"He's a D'Shan isn't he?" The old lady brushed a couple of crumbs absent-mindedly from her lap. "Of course he has the Gift. He's turned to the bad, that young man. Thinks he has all the power in the world! Humph! He thought to get his hands on this place. He won't be back though, I soon told him what I thought of him." Eleanor saw the girls' horrified expressions. "Don't look so alarmed children! Elaine, do you think you are the first to have the Gift in our family? Where did you think it came from? Not your mother or your father! The Gift often skips a generation."

"You have the Gift too?" Elaine exclaimed.

"Of course I have! I've never troubled much with it though. Not my thing. I had been expecting Tristan ever since Master Berant came to see me on his way up to that school of yours a month or so ago."

"You know Master Berant?" Lydia managed to ask first.

"Since he was a boy," Eleanor replied. "He used to put in for stores at Whellan. Many's the time we fitted him out with provisions and cordage; sails and the like. He was for ever off on some journey or another. Oh yes, we go back aways. I had quite a chat with him. I can't say that I approve of the way the Mageseekers terrify the wits out of young and old alike, whatever their reasons might be. As if the Gift was something to be afraid of. I told him so! I said that I didn't expect him to come it the high and mighty over my granddaughter, what with us being old friends." The two girls gaped.

"That's why he didn't let them take me!" Elaine said.

"You'll go yourself, in your own time, like I told him," the old lady stated firmly.

"He said his was the harder course to steer. Do you know what he meant by that?" Elaine asked. Eleanor D'Shan chuckled as she helped herself to a slice of cake before passing the plate round to the girls.

"He talks in riddles, doesn't he? It makes him seem clever and mysterious, so he reckons! He means, dear, that you can go to the Navigator's Guild on Forath for the first part of your training."

"The Navigators!" Elaine's whole face lit up with excitement. "I never realised!"

"Why Elaine, what do you think the Navigators and Weatherworkers are but Sea Mages? Master Berant himself is a member of both Guilds and one of their most powerful members I should imagine, though like most men he lacks basic sense. He should stand up to those fools at the Kerun Dur and I told him so!"

The thought of Master Berant being given a sound ticking off by Eleanor D'Shan brought a smile to both girls' faces which they quickly smothered. "I hear your father's in a spot of trouble," Eleanor continued suddenly, turning to face Lydia. "Always was a weak fool and now what's to come of this I can't tell." Lydia shifted awkwardly, embarrassed by the brutal frankness of her Great Aunt's words.

The elder Mrs D'Shan stared hard at Lydia for a moment as if thinking deeply. Lydia got the distinct impression that she was being appraised by the shrewd old lady in front of her. "I shall think about what's for the best," Eleanor said eventually. "The last thing you need is a hasty and ill-considered marriage, which is no doubt what your mother is presently planning on Thirnmar. The D'Shan's are strongest when they marry for love, not money or position. Your father would have done well to remember that although he undoubtedly does care for your mother.

Now unless girls are very much changed from when I was young, you both have good appetites. There is plenty of cake and more tea in the pot."

With that, Eleanor changed the subject of the conversation to lighter matters. Further talk of the Gift or Lydia's fortunes was not encouraged. Instead both girls listened to the old lady's memories and tales of her home; the large island kingdom of Wheldor some distance to their Est. It was approaching five o'clock when Eleanor rose to her feet and announced that she was going to prepare for the Harvest Home. "Mr Brown will take care of you both.

The coachman appeared, seemingly summoned by telepathy, at the door and ushered them through a maze of corridors in the servants' part of the house to the kitchens which were a hive of activity. The girls were assaulted by steam, bustle and cooking smells but Mr Brown didn't give them time to linger. Instead he rushed them through the back door into a yard at the rear of the manor. From there he hurried them on out of the chill wind to the largest coach house through whose partially open doors light and laughter spilled in equal measure.

Inside, the space had been cleared and two long tables laid out. A makeshift stage had been created at one end by using hay bales with planks rested across them. On it, a small band was tuning its instruments. The beams, chairs and walls were decorated with flowers and greenery in addition to elaborately plaited sheaves of corn. This method of decoration was a Forngarth tradition and one of which the estate was proud.

Since festivities were due to start at Five, the space was already crowded with estate's labourers and their families on one table and the tenant farmers, their families and more senior workers on the second. Elaine and Lydia were shown to seats on this latter table. Both felt slightly awkward as the men touched their forelocks respectfully to them but the moment passed.

The assembled company took their seats and the band struck up with a lively tune. The first of the kitchen staff entered and began laying out the feast. This took a while as there was a great deal to lay out: freshly baked rolls, game pie, tureens of soup, fruit, vegetables and every manner of dish that Forngarth's kitchen could create was first placed on the table and then generously served out to the company. Wine was served on the top table and cider on the lower. Voices grew louder, as did the laughter, whilst the general spirit of the room lifted.

This was the purpose of the holiday and at each estate on the island, and on each independent farm, similar feasts took place over the three-week period according to local custom. Alongside these were village fairs and other communal events to mark the turning of the season and the provision of a good harvest against the winter months. Neither girl could recall attending this type of feast before. In Lydia's case this was because Wescliffe didn't have any tenant farmers. Besides, her parents had heard that the occasions were rowdy affairs unsuitable for their daughter. In Elaine's case it was because her life revolved around the sea rather than the land.

After much of the food had been eaten, an expectant hush descended over the company. Staff from the house bustled around the tables charging everyone's glasses. Lydia had been cautious with the wine, a result of her experience in Perth Cathe which she had no wish to repeat. Elaine had drunk a couple of glasses and was flushed with the excitement and atmosphere of the room.

The door opened and Eleanor D'Shan entered slowly and with great dignity. As one, the company rose to their feet. The men touched their forelocks while the women bobbed or curtseyed. Eleanor rested heavily on her cane as she walked but her back was straight and she acknowledged many of those she passed with a slight nod of recognition and pleasure.

She had dressed herself with care for the occasion and though her dress was mostly black once again, it was decorated with pearl details and small diamond shards that shimmered as she moved. Her hair was fashionably tied up and fastened with a silver tiara. Mr Brown assisted his mistress onto the stage where she turned to face the room. A wave of her hand was the cue for everyone to be seated.

"By tradition and with thanks I welcome you all to Forngarth. Through your labours we have had a good harvest this year." There was a murmur of agreement from the room. "Your families will be well provided for in the months ahead and it is with pride that I can say for the fourth year in succession, each of our tenants has seen an improved yield. This means that each farm will receive the appropriate additional payment for all staff." There was a hearty cheer at this. Eleanor smiled and there was genuine warmth in her eyes as she looked about her. "My late husband was proud of this estate and the people who work it. I share that pride as should you all. Before the tables are cleared and the dance can begin I have one final duty to attend to. Please stand and raise your glasses for the toasts. Firstly, to the Harvest Home!"

"The Harvest Home!" The assembled company responded with a will, raising their glasses and drinking.

"And secondly, to the King!"

"The King! Long live the King!" This was delivered with even more gusto. Caught in the moment, Elaine and Lydia raised their own voices also. Once the King's health had been drunk, one of the farmers cleared his throat nervously.

"By your leave, Lady D'Shan, it falls to me to thank you on behalf of us all for this feast and for your patronage. There isn't a man or woman here who isn't thankful to be part of the Forngarth estate." There was a chorus of "ayes" to this. "So, if I may be so bold, I offer another toast. To Forngarth!"

"Forngarth!" This final shout fairly rattled the rafters. A voice from the lower table called out.

"Three cheers for her Ladyship! Hip, Hip!"

"Huzzah! Huzzah! Huzzuah!" The cheers were delivered in quick succession as was the custom, followed by enthusiastic applause. Eleanor appeared to be genuinely moved and smiled warmly.

"Thank you. Thank you all. Now I shall detain you no longer. As soon as the tables are cleared, the harvest dance may commence!"

With many willing hands it did not take long for the space to be cleared. The tables were folded and carried outside. The chairs were placed around the edge of the room. Eleanor retired to the main house despite requests for her to remain. She told the girls the festivities would be less restrained without her presence. "Be sure to enjoy yourselves you two but I can't have you home too late or my daughter will have words to say to me! Mr Brown will keep an eye on things and let you know when it is time to leave. I have enjoyed seeing you both."

"Thank you Grandma," Elaine replied and was permitted to deliver a kiss on the cheek.

"Thank you, Great Aunt." Lydia curtseyed gracefully, receiving another approving nod. Shortly afterwards the dance began.

This was not a dance in the sense that Miss Drake would have recognised the term. The steps were not those the girls had learned at school, which for the most part had involved demure circles at a discreet distance from the dance partner. These may have been designed for occasions with wide skirts and corsets (which, since they prevented breathing or any exertion, precluded anything more energetic). The music here was that of the countryside. Fiddle, drum and accordion seemed to compete to deliver the fastest beat. There appeared to be no protocol for inviting dance partners either, much to the girl's bemusement. As the tune got going, they were each plucked from their seats by a suitable young farmer and drawn into the circle of dancers.

The trick, Lydia quickly found, was to ignore her feet altogether and allow herself to skip and circle according to the tune. Indeed, the less she thought about what she was doing the easier it became. Glancing across she could see Elaine was also getting the hang of things. Occasionally, when the whirlwind brought them close together, Elaine flashed her cousin a happy smile before being drawn away again.

The music, the dance and the laughing company completely absorbed Lydia, lifting her spirits in a way they had never been before. Despite the fact that her male dance partners (these changed regularly as the dance wore on) had been well indulged with drink there was never a hint of any disrespect or misbehaviour. The whole occasion, though apparently one of amiable anarchy, was governed by well understood rules and customs. Both girls cast their recent cares aside and allowed themselves to enjoy the moment.

It was late when Lydia and Elaine were bundled back into the coach for long journey back to TolSor. Both had already slept in the coach by the time the tower's flashing light, lit by Elaine's mother, welcomed them back to their beds.

Neither girl could have seen the concealed figure who watched them step down from the coach and enter the welcoming light of TolSor's front door. With a satisfied smile, the shadowy figure slipped back to where his horse was tethered and galloped away towards Perth Cathe.

Chapter Ten - Storm Clouds

The girls had not long departed for Forngarth when a horse and rider galloped up to TolSor's back door. The rider dismounted, banged twice on the door and let himself in. Sasha looked up from nursing the baby, surprised but not alarmed. After the briefest of pauses her face broke into a welcoming smile.

"Edward! What a wonderful surprise." The welcome died on her lips, however, as she saw the old sailor's grim expression. "What is it?"

"Business visit I'm afraid, Ma'am. Is Dan awake?"

"I expect so, go through." Shasha's tone was rather cooler now. Edward ignored it and strode into the darkened bedroom where his old friend was lying weakly in bed.

"Dan!" he greeted deeply. "No mate, don't stir. I'll not keep you but a minute; there are things we need to talk about. There have been questions asked at The Mermaid and if I'm any judge there's trouble brewing. We'd best think how to deal with it. The girls are away today?" Dan nodded. "That's well," Edward continued, "gives us a chance to talk."

Edward stayed only a short time at TolSor. On his way out, he made his peace with Sasha. "There's not much to be done but stay alert," he said finally. "I'll round up a few lads in the next day or so and we'll set things to rights. Meantime, keep the girls close and lock your doors o' nights. It's just for a couple of days Ma'am, that's all."

"You're very kind Edward and a good friend to us," Sasha told him. She had paced nervously round the house until the girls' safe return. Even when they were asleep and Dan was snoring loudly beside her Sasha remained on edge and awake. A gnawing anxiety refused to let her be; a sense of some unseen danger close by.

The following morning was the same as the one before it. TolSor was very much a place of routine. Lydia was pleased to find herself awake once again at the same time as Elaine without needing her cousin to shake her. Indeed, it seemed that Elaine was the worse of the two of them for the previous night's revelries.

They climbed the tower and once Elaine had dowsed the lamp they wound the weights. Having completed the winding, along with the by now traditional complaints and whinges, Lydia was expecting to head back down for breakfast but Elaine had other ideas.

"I want to go back up to the roof," she said. "You'd better come too." They climbed the winding stair and emerged into ice cold air and bright sunlight.

"What a day!" Lydia exclaimed. "Do you think we'll have time to go for a walk? I'd love to look at those old towers."

"I'm not sure..." Elaine's voice trailed off as she shaded her eyes with her hands, looking off into the distance.

"What is it?" Lydia knew her cousin well enough to spot that there was something troubling her.

"What do you make of that?" Elaine pointed in the direction of Thirnmar. She was leaning out across the stonework next to the small "hut" from which the staircase emerged.

"What?" Lydia repeated, not seeing anything at first, then: "Oh." Far away, beyond the low hump of Thirnmar's headlands, part of the skyline was dark as if smudged with charcoal.

"Wind's light," Elaine was thinking aloud.

"But it's from the Sor-Wes," Lydia finished the thought. "And it can strengthen quickly enough." They exchanged a look. The girls knew well the changeable nature of weather in each season, both living so close to the sea. Clouds like that at this time of year could only mean one thing.

"I'd better talk to Father," Elaine said suddenly, making a decision. "It looks like we're going to be busy. We'll have to keep watch up here today. Tower regulations say that someone has to be on watch if the weather looks like turning nasty. If it blows up the way I think it's going to, one or other of us will be out here in some pretty nasty weather." Elaine was worried. "You stay up here for now, I'll bring food up. You need to let me know as soon as you see any ships. I'm not talking about the fishing boats – they know the signs well enough – I'm talking about the merchantmen or navy ships. I'll be back soon." With that Elaine was gone, running down the stairs like the wind.

Before knocking at her father's door, Elaine decided to get a second opinion. "Mother! Can you come outside for a minute? I don't like the look of the weather." With a nod Sasha hurried outside. The dark smudge was just about visible from ground level.

"Go wake your father," Sasha said immediately.

Father was not looking any better thought Elaine, as she told him the news. For a second he looked as though he were going to get out of bed. He half threw the cover aside and went to swing his feet out but his strength failed. He sank back with a pained gasp.

"I'm done in!" he exclaimed with a curse. "Damned lot of use I am!"

"Lydia and I will help, Father," Elaine said quietly. "Just tell me what you want us to do."

"Set the flag first. Man the tower and warn any shipping. How are we for oil?"

"Three fresh jars. We raised them yesterday," Elaine told her father, thanking providence that she'd decided not to put that job off. Bad weather from the Sor-Wes tended to mean a blow and it was no joke operating the crane in high wind.

"Good lass." Dan was impressed. "Light the lamp at the first sign of visibility dropping. You know the rule, haze over Krann Headland. Keep me informed, would you? And ask your mother to step in and see me a minute."

Elaine bounded breathlessly back up the stairs clutching a bundle hastily pulled from a cupboard by the tower's front door. She found Lydia staring intently to the Est.

"There's a four-master out there," Lydia reported. "Only just come into view. Not navy."

"Right!" Elaine said grimly. "Give us a hand here, Lydia. Untie those halliards." A tall flagpole was bolted to the wall of the "hut". The girls made the flag fast and ran it up where, once clear of the roof, it broke free and flapped heavily; a massive flag of blood-red. The message was clear enough: DANGER! "Have they seen it?" Elaine asked. There was a fair swell and the ship was difficult to make out, being partially shrouded in its own spray. The two girls watched attentively for an anguished couple of minutes but the distant speck continued to butt into the swell as it tacked down Carras Sound towards them. "This is your chance, girl!" Elaine said eventually, breaking into a grin. "Give them a blast on the horn."

"Me? Really?" Lydia fairly leapt towards the stairs.

"You have to wind pretty fast," Elaine warned. "Once you start, keep at it. It won't work otherwise."

"Sure!" Lydia was gone. Elaine chuckled to herself, turning back towards the ship. She knew well enough that the novelty would wear off pretty quickly. It had for her.

Below, Lydia scrambled onto the box and took a careful grasp of the brass handle. Placing her feet carefully, and taking a deep breath, she began to wind. There was an initial resistance before the machine began to gather speed. Lydia suspected that the fan was attached to a heavy flywheel. As the speed picked up it became easier. She wound furiously, wondering if anything was ever going to happen.

It started as a faint hum in the wooden case next to her. It deepened to a thrum, growing in volume. Suddenly the horn found its resonance and the trumpet part began to sound. The very room itself vibrated with a deafening deep boom which rattled inside Lydia's lungs for twenty long seconds before she let go of the handle which continued to turn. It slowed gradually as the deep note died away. "Gosh!" Lydia said to the empty room. Then she ran upstairs.

"They heard that alright! Look." Elaine pointed up Carras Sound. The distant ship had turned full about and was spreading every sail she could carry. "They'll be snug in Nellad Bay before this lot blows up!" Elaine had taken a huge telescope from its shelf in the lamp room and was watching the distant speck. She turned from time to time to scan the rest of the Sound as well as the Cathe. "Hullo! Our friends on Elledran have woken up at last. There goes their flag."

"Could I look?" Lydia took the offered telescope and peered along the bearing Elaine gave her. On the distant shore a building similar to their own had hoisted a red flag.

"Can you see the one on Thirnmar?" Elaine asked. Lydia turned.

"Can't make it out," she said eventually. "It's gone hazy over that way; the wind must be getting up."

"I'm lighting the lamp," Elaine said suddenly remembering her father's instructions. "We've plenty of oil." The lamp took only a little time to light. When she came back, Lydia's first words stunned her.

"Will SKYLARK be all right do you think?" Elaine was momentarily struck dumb. She was supposed to be the sailor and yet she hadn't so much as thought about their little boat all morning.

"We'll shift her in a bit. The cov's well sheltered for a blow from the Sor-Wes but better safe than sorry. I'll have to ask Mother to keep watch while we shift her; can't leave the tower unmanned with the flag flying. I won't bother her now as we've a good few hours yet. Best keep our eyes peeled."

Four more times that morning Lydia dived below to sound the foghorn to warn off ships. On the last occasion the wind had begun to freshen and was carrying the first hint of rain. The last of the ships was small and when Lydia returned to the roof she found Elaine staring at it intently.

"That ship seems familiar somehow," she said. "You take a look." Lydia found that the ship was clearly in focus. It was much closer than the previous three, as it was rounding the point from Perth Cathe, rather than sailing down Carras Sound as the others had been.

"They'd be better turning back I should think," Lydia said. "It can't be more than an hour back to Perth Cathe. Oh! That's where we saw her, you remember? The sailor chap said she's from Wheldor. Sheer-something her name is. They don't look as though they're turning back to me though. They just set their topsails!"

"Fools! They'll not outrun the weather in that little ship, they haven't the speed. They'll get themselves wrecked on Carran Thum likely enough!" Elaine was angry at the stupidity of the ship's captain, whoever he was. What was the point of warning towers if they were ignored? But the small ship surprised her. It appeared to heel suddenly and the sails were trimmed as if to catch a strong breeze from the Nor-Wes. The ship surged forwards, casting up a huge bow wave as it began to move rapidly up Carras Sound towards TolSor.

"What?" Elaine could scarcely find words. The ship was defying every rule of sailing.

"Heavens!" Lydia exclaimed suddenly. "They must have a Weatherworker aboard. I've heard they can change the wind at will. I've never seen it done before though. It's the only explanation."

"They'll get well clear, that's for sure," Elaine said, her voice full of awe. "If there's a Weatherworker aboard, they won't fear any storm so long as the ship's clear of land. Hullo! They're saluting!" Both girls saw the black and yellow flag at the schooner's stern drop and rise in the universal salute. By agreement, the girls rushed to the halliards and returned the gesture with their own flag. They watched the small vessel race into the distance until Sasha arrived to allow them to attend to SKYLARK.

There was little to be done, in practical terms, but the jobs were time consuming. The girls used the anchors to warp SKYLARK closer to the shelter of the high ground up-wind of the boat's present anchorage. Elaine and Lydia worked steadily as a team but it was hard going. Once that job had been completed, both girls went over the whole boat carefully. They double-checked that everything was lashed down tightly including the canvas cover over the cockpit; neither girl particularly liked bailing and there would be a good deal of rainfall overnight they judged.

The girls climbed the uneven path back up to the tower about an hour and a half later, happy that their boat would ride out the coming weather safely enough. They were about to head around the back of the house to the kitchen when Elaine suddenly caught a glimpse of movement by the tower.

"Hey!" she called immediately and ran to the corner. Lydia was just a few steps behind, although she hadn't seen anything herself. They rounded the corner at the run and almost collided with the man who was standing there. He was a rough-looking fellow; unshaven with an unkempt beard and poor clothes. "What's your business here?" Elaine's challenge was confident and assured. This was her home and this man was not dangerous like Groth, nor Tristan.

"I've a message for Dan Sheldon. We're coming tonight." The man leered at Elaine, bringing his face close to hers. His teeth were rotten and his breath was almost overpowering. "Tell him, won't you, love? It's tonight. Your little hiding place is known!" Elaine's hand flashed around like lightening, striking the man a terrific slap on his cheek. He started back in surprise and pain.

"Go to hell!" Elaine snapped.

"That one's for free." The man's voice was sullen. "You'll get what's coming. I know a man who's been looking for you and your friend here." All the while he had been backing away as Elaine walked slowly forward, her whole being trembling with pure rage. As she drew level with the door to the piggery behind the tower, she picked up the mucking-out shovel and hefted it in her hands.

"I'm gone," the man said. "But you'll be seeing me again," he added darkly before turning away.

"Heavens, Elaine!" Lydia exclaimed eventually. This was a whole side of her cousin she'd only glimpsed briefly before; the fiery temper which flared without warning. Usually it was directed at Mary Newton and her cronies but that had been just a shadow of the rage which was now subsiding. Elaine carefully replaced the shovel.

Elaine quickly checked that everything was in place before locking the door to the piggery and pocketing the key. Whatever else he might be the man was evidently not a thief but that was no excuse to take chances.

"You'd best go up the tower," she said to Lydia. Her voice had a faint tremor. "We promised Mother we'd relieve her as soon as we'd finished with SKYLARK. I'm going to talk to Father."

Rain was falling as fine spray by the time Elaine re-joined Lydia on the roof of TolSor. This made the wind, which was strengthening steadily, seem a great deal colder.

"Mother's packing in the house," she told Lydia. "We're going to move into the tower. We don't usually bother this early in the season but, well..."

"Better safe than sorry," Lydia agreed thinking about the stout doors. "What did your father say?"

"Not a lot really. He isn't at all well. He seems to be getting worse, though Mother says not to worry. The fever will run its course, she says."

The two girls huddled in their waterproofs in what little shelter was offered by the "hut". It was now late afternoon and clouds covered the sky bringing an early twilight. As yet it was low cover; the really dark stuff remained a threatening menace on the horizon. White caps were visible in the slowly rising swell out to sea but for the time being there were no ships to be seen. They kept watch together for forty minutes before a grinding noise below their feet announced the fact that the last of the weights had reached the floor, stalling the rotating screen mechanism for the lamp.

"Twice in one day!" Lydia grumped for both of them as they descended the stairs to attend to the problem. They tossed for who would wind first and Elaine won (again) prompting a further torrent of good natured whinging from Lydia which put a smile on Elaine's face for the first time since their encounter with the stranger.

They had an early tea at half past five in the room on the ground floor of the tower. Many of the family's belongings had been brought in already and the fire was beginning to take the chill off the room. After tea, the girls were expecting to return to their vigil on the roof but Elaine's mother had other ideas.

"Lydia, dear, I need you to bring in a good supply of logs from around the back. There's a basket by the kitchen door."

"Of course, Aunt Sasha," Lydia headed straight out to the kitchen to get started, grabbing her waterproof cloak as she went. Next Sasha turned to her daughter.

"I want you to move some of those big storage boxes in front of the door there. Stack 'em right up close to the door then ask Lydia to stack the firewood in front of them. Just in case, love," she added, catching Elaine's alarmed expression. "I'm going to move David's crib upstairs now, then I'll shift your father."

When Lydia returned, struggling under the weight of a large basket of logs, she found the construction of the barricade well under way. Two heavy general stores boxes were placed right up against the solid door which had also been secured by a heavy bar. Elaine had decided to reinforce this with the heaviest of the crates left behind by the builders. Unfortunately, she wasn't having much luck moving it.

"I don't suppose you'd like a hand at all?" Lydia enquired sweetly having watched her cousin turn purple with the effort. Elaine collapsed with a gasp.

"Wouldn't say no," she agreed. "I don't know what's in this thing but it weighs at least a couple of tons!" This was an exaggeration but the spare iron weight was certainly very heavy. Between them, the girls moved it into place.

"That ought to do the trick!" Lydia observed between puffs as they caught their breath.

"I should think so. Um…" Elaine stood and crossed the room to where the box had originally stood. "There's another trap door here," she said pointing.

"And?" Lydia was surprised by Elaine's reaction. It was, after all, more or less below the others. "Surely this place has a basement?"

"Actually, no!" Elaine said, kneeling and peering closely at the grubby wooden square set in the floor. "This tower has solid foundations. The builders were worried about subsidence. I'm sure this wasn't here last holiday. Father made me clean in here when I cracked the window in my room. I'd have seen this for sure."

"Maybe the builders added it?"

"Why, I wonder? I'm going to have a look." The ring embedded in the door was easy enough to lift. Lydia lent her strength as soon as she could get a grip and the door creaked open heavily, showering dust over the pair. "Fetch the lamp would you?" Elaine couldn't make anything out in the gloom.

The relatively small amount of light cast by the table lamp revealed a small pit beneath the floor. It was crammed with more crates and boxes similar to those they had used to barricade the door. "Just stores." Elaine's voice rang with disappointment. Treasure would have been better.

"Better get on with things," Lydia said suddenly. "Your mother wanted several baskets of wood brought in."

"You're right," Elaine agreed as she let the door fall back into place, "and we haven't checked topside for a while." As if to reinforce the point a sudden hard gust of wind whistled around the tower.

Elaine helped her mother get David's crib up the narrow staircase to the bedroom whilst Lydia continued to bring in enough firewood to keep both fires alight for a couple of days if needed. Her mother again stopped her going up to the roof, asking instead that she go and see her father.

Dan looked terrible in the flickering candlelight but he interrupted Elaine's expression of concern sharply.

"No time, girl. Here's the key to the trunk by the window. You know what's inside. Move everything into the tower. You can leave it all on the table for now. We won't be sitting down to a meal until the morning by my guess." Elaine took the offered key and moved to a large, very solid, iron-bound trunk beneath the window next to the bed. The key turned easily enough but the lid required some effort to open. Inside was a large bundle wrapped in cloth. Metal gleamed at one end and from the other projected three ash stocks.

Without comment, Elaine gathered the heavy bundle up and returned to the tower passing her mother on the way. Usually Sasha was nervous of the guns and had complained on numerous occasions about having such things under her roof. Today she nodded in understanding as they passed; a gesture which chilled Elaine with sudden apprehension. Her parents were behaving as though the wreckers were still abroad. In the early days of TolSor, the keeper and his wife had often had to fight off groups of men and women determined to dowse the light and offer their own "guide" to ships in trouble. That had been hundreds of years ago. Threatening though the man's message had been, surely no one would be coming to trouble TolSor on a night such as this promised to be?

The wind was by now gusting regularly around the tower. It echoed in the chimneys and even sometimes caused an odd hollow whine from the foghorn when it blew just so. It was an unpleasant, haunting noise which had scared Elaine often in her childhood. Now the association of those fears, mingled with the stress of the moment, made her shiver.

Elaine opened the bundle and set each musket out on the table in a row, quickly inspecting the flints. One looked as though it might need some work. The muskets appeared to be free of rust, which was good, and each had a small pouch of ammunition. What she didn't have, Elaine realised quickly, were the powder horns that went with each piece. They were kept in pockets inside the lid of the trunk and she had forgotten to remove them. Elaine made her way back to her parents' room to collect them.

The wind was louder still in the house, rattling windows and causing her bedroom door to bang in the draught. These sounds combined to mask her approach and she arrived at the door just as Sasha was lifting Dan from the bed. Sasha had her head bowed as her husband looped his arm across her shoulder for support. He had his back to the door and didn't see Elaine standing there.

Her father's nightshirt tangled as he stood, rising to expose his back. It revealed a swathe of bandage about his chest below the armpits. Between the shoulder blades was a wide, circular, crimson stain; unmistakably a wound and only one sort of wound bled like that. With a short gasp, Elaine pulled away from the doorway and ran back to the tower, tears welling in her eyes. She stood for a second before grabbing the lamp from the table and crossing to the trap door in the floor.

Perhaps the door was easier to move this time, or perhaps the shock lent her strength, but in any case it was open in a moment. She lay on the floor and, clasping the lamp in one hand, leant down into the pit recklessly. She scanned the crates quickly, knowing what she was looking for and not finding it. None of the crates bore the black crown mark indicating cargo on which revenue had been paid. This was contraband!

When her parents came through to the tower with Sasha supporting a weak and stumbling Dan the trap door was shut. Elaine was at the table with her back to them working on the flint. As their footsteps receded up the stairs, Elaine returned to collect the powder horns. She gathered them in her arms but before she could turn she was overcome by emotion. She stood swaying, her shoulders shaking with sobs as tears streamed down her cheeks. In her mind's eye a single image replayed over and over again: that of the man on the beach throwing up his arms and falling to musket fire.

When Elaine joined Lydia on the roof she had regained her composure but was cold and distant in response to Lydia's remarks about the worsening weather. She turned from her and busied herself in the lamp room, topping up the reservoir and generally fussing about. Lydia was bemused by this sudden change in her cousin but decided to let the matter rest for now. Her attention was occupied by the weather.

Heavy rain was now lashing the island accompanied by a wind that was strong and rising but also prone to sudden fierce blasts. Over Thirnmar lighting flickered occasionally accompanied by distant rumbles of thunder. The sea was making its power felt now; pounding the coast below TolSor and sending up great geysers of spray across the headland. None of the fury found its way into the cov, Lydia noticed, and SKYLARK seemed to be riding it out quite comfortably. Which is more, Lydia thought grimly, than can be said for me!

Elaine emerged from the lamp room eventually but even then she scarcely acknowledged Lydia, preferring instead to stand a short distance away. Elaine stared moodily out into the gathering darkness as the storm's overture played out before her. It was both terrifying in its power and beautiful in its spectacle. After ten long minutes of standing in silence, Elaine turned suddenly and moved towards the door. This was too much for Lydia who grabbed her arm.

"Elaine, what's the matter? Are you all right?" Elaine shook her head.

"Not now, Lydia. There's something I've got to do..." she broke free from her cousin's grasp and ran from her down the stairs to the sleeping level.

She entered quietly, not wishing to disturb the baby who had finally dropped off to sleep. The move had drawn heavily on her father's limited reserve of strength. The wound was bleeding again and the pain in his chest was considerable. It was affecting his breathing which came in short shallow gasps. Dan opened his eyes and saw his daughter standing before him with a determined expression on her face. The similarity to her mother was most striking. Dan smiled weakly.

"What's up, lass?" How do I begin? Elaine wondered. She decided to just say what was on her mind

"I know, Father. I found the contraband."

"Ah." Dan patted the bed and waited for Elaine to sit while he mustered his thoughts. "I Just store the stuff, dear," he began, but Elaine cut him off angrily.

"Don't lie to me, father! We were there, Lydia and I, on the ridge behind the beach. We saw everything. All those soldiers who died. All those men! I saw you fall. It was Edward who came back for you, wasn't it?" Elaine had given the matter some thought. Edward was certainly not above a bit of smuggling. He was also the only person she could think of who would do something so brave as to go back for a friend under fire. "Why, Father? It's so dangerous! You could have been killed!"

"We need the money dear. My allowance for this place barely keeps us in food and clothing. The fishing hasn't been so good lately and there's the baby to think of. I want better than this for you, child. You deserve more. Your mother married below herself. I should never have asked such a thing of her but I was young and a fool."

"You were in love and you still are. Both of you! You should marry for love," Elaine repeated the advice of her grandmother. "We get by, don't we? Nothing's worth the risk. What would we do if you are taken and hanged? Why take such a chance?" Elaine repeated, angry at her father for risking everything for a few crates of smuggled goods.

"Your schooling dear," Dan responded gently. "Where did you think the money came from, eh? We've never had a penny from Forngarth, you know that."

"School?" Elaine was aghast. "Father, I hate the place! I've never asked to go, I never expected to! I certainly didn't want this! How could you?" She burst into tears. It was true that she hadn't given any thought to where the money came from. Perhaps a part of me has always known I wouldn't like the answer she admitted truthfully to herself. But it had seemed important to her parents and so, despite the misery of being away from home and having to endure the company of girls who constantly put her down, she had gone. She had made the best of it, she knew, working hard even at those classes for which she had no ability whatsoever.

"Elaine," her father's cold, weak hand touched her cheek. "Don't take on lass, I can't bear it." There were tears in his eyes too as he sought the words to explain and to make amends. "You're a young lady now. You could better yourself. Be whatever you want. Marry whoever you want... you understand? Your connection to Forngarth, the money that will one day be yours, counts for nothing without schooling. Your mother and I have always known this. We want you to have the choice, lass, to become whatever you choose. The stars alone know how proud I am of you. You'd make a fine tower keeper, or woman of business, or Lady-of-the-Manor. Whatever you become, I'll be the proudest man on the island. But I had to get you schooling, love, so as you could choose your path for yourself. You see?" Elaine nodded.

"Then it's my fault you're hurt."

"NO!" Dan's voice strengthened to something of its normal tone. "I make my own mistakes, our girl. Should've steered well clear that night. I had a feeling all was not well but what with the new term starting and all... Anyway, I chose how to pay the fees didn't I? I knew what was at stake as we all did. But no more. You're right, my love, there's no call to go risking everything. I'll pay the fees another way – an honest man's way."

"How?"

"Damned if I know," he responded with a shadow of a grin, "but we Sheldons always come up with something. It's not just you and your mother who got the brains in this family, though I'll allow you have a deal more common sense at times. There are a few things I could try."

"You're not to get a loan from anyone," Elaine ordered. "I've heard tell about the sort of people who lend money. We don't need to deal with those people!"

"Don't worry, lass. I'll find a better way than that." Dan was actually wondering whether he might lease out his beloved fishing boat to someone in Perth Cathe. He didn't say this as he knew that Elaine would forbid that too and refuse to go to school as likely as not.

"Now, since you know most of it, I'd best tell you the rest," Dan continued. "We were set up, lass, so was Lydia's father and by the same man I'd wager. Me and the lads, well, we don't take too kindly to that treatment. We've decided to sell the stuff on ourselves. We paid dearly enough for it after all. There are several families in need of support now with their men gone.

They brought me back here on the cart and put the goods in the storage cell downstairs. Somehow, and by the heavens if I find out how there'll be an extra grave to dig, our usual contacts have discovered the stuff's here. Edward'll sort them out but he needs time to round up a crew to see them off. Until then, it's just us. We might have company tonight. I'd let them take the stuff but they're not the sort to forget the insult. Make no mistake, dear, they'll be after our lives. It's the sort of men they are. You may have to use those muskets. Whatever happens they mustn't get in! Not with you ladies in the place. Can you be strong for me?"

"Of course, Father. I should tell Lydia though. She's in as much danger as the rest of us."

"I'd rather you didn't, love. Her father, see?"

"Lydia's no snitch, really Father! 'Sides, Mr D'Shan's not going to be Revenue Officer for much longer. I don't think he's been entirely honest himself. Lydia's one of us, Father. She's put herself at risk for me once already. I can't be dishonest to her now."

"Very well. Just one thing, lass, before you go." Dan clasped his daughter's hand tightly, his eyes bored into hers as he spoke from the heart. "I acted for the best. Not wisely, I'll grant you, but for the best. Forgive me and please don't think less of me." Elaine's eyes filled with tears again and they embraced.

"I could never do that Father," she said softly. "Of course I forgive you."

Chapter Eleven - The Storm Breaks

When Elaine emerged back onto the roof she found that her cousin had been transformed into a hunched and bedraggled figure. The wind was continuing to rise but it was now raining in earnest, lancing out of the darkness. The sensation, after only a few seconds, was very much like taking a wash under the pump. The large ice-cold drops stung any exposed skin and made her eyes smart.

"Nothing in sight," Lydia reported. "Mind you, I can't see all that far and the telescope's no use in this."

"I'm sorry about just now," Elaine said sincerely.

"Are you all right now?" Lydia asked.

"Pretty much, thanks. Look, I think you've earned a hot drink. Let's go in for a bit. I need to tell you a few things. I'm sure Mother won't mind a short spell on watch."

Warm tea was indeed most welcome. The girls sat in front of the fire drinking out of large mugs and, in Lydia's case, steaming gently. It took a good few minutes for Elaine to explain the situation to her cousin. Despite her earlier comments to her father Elaine was anxious when, finally, she completed her account. Lydia was silent, staring into the fire as her mind raced.

First, Lydia quickly reviewed the story piecing all the elements of what Elaine had told her with what she had already guessed about her father's dealings at Wescliffe. Only then did Lydia consider her own feelings. In much the same way that Elaine had been reared with a hatred of wreckers, so Lydia's view of smugglers was highly influenced by her father's job. She was slightly shocked to discover that she was staying in the home of a smuggler. Yet now was not the time to give in to prejudice. There were more immediate concerns.

"It seems to me," Lydia said eventually, "that our fathers have both been more involved in smuggling than is good for them! I'm hardly in a position to get all moral on the subject am I? How likely is it those men will come here tonight do you think?"

"If I were them, in this weather, I'd not bother," Elaine replied, "but Father seems to think it likely and he's the one who knows them."

"Well, you might want to show me how to reload a musket," Lydia suggested grimly. "I doubt I'd be able to fire one without blowing myself up but I could reload for you if it comes to it."

"Right." Elaine stood and they moved together to the kitchen table. She reached for a musket but before picking it up looked Lydia squarely in the eye. "Thanks, Lydia."

"Don't thank me yet!" Lydia protested. "I'm about as much good with this sort of thing as you are at tapestry!"

"That wasn't what I meant."

"I know," Lydia became serious for a moment. "We seem to get into these situations lately don't we? Best stick together I reckon. Now, which end goes bang again?" Elaine had to smile. Either Lydia was refusing to acknowledge the danger they might be in or she was being incredibly brave. Experience told her it was probably the latter.

Fifteen minutes later, Lydia could prime and reload a musket although she was slower than either girl would have liked. Just in case, Elaine took her through the motions of firing the thing as well but they agreed this was best avoided. All three pieces were now primed and loaded, though the triggers were only half-cocked. The girls were considering going up to relieve Sasha when the evening was rent by a deafening clap of thunder. The girls headed immediately for the stairs. By the time they reached the next floor, David was protesting loudly in his crib at this interruption to his slumber. Elaine paused in her climb to thrust him into the surprised arms of her father before continuing up to the roof.

The weather had turned dramatic both girls saw at once. The wind had increased to the point that it made a continuous wailing sound as it blew around the tower. At sea the waves looked treacherous indeed with powerful, steep-sided waves creating dangerous areas of confused currents. Nearer to shore, away from the conflicting influences of the Cathe and Carras Sound, the waves became deadlier still. They were mounting in height and driving relentlessly onto the coast with explosive force. The pounding of the waves was echoed, periodically, by loud rumbles of thunder close by as lightning stabbed down from the sky above.

"David?" Sasha shouted to make herself heard.

"With Father!" Elaine yelled back. "Any ships?"

"None that I can see!" Sasha reported. The rain limited visibility most of the time, as did the veil of spray rising along the shoreline, but the lightening compensated for this by giving them brief glimpses of the sea in its terrible fury. No ship could be seen, which was just as well. Any vessel out in those seas would need much more than a light to guarantee its safety. The intervention of a powerful Weatherworker might just save them but little else.

The three huddled against the wind together as the rain became mixed with the first few hail stones to add to their misery. For some reason, Sasha was unwilling to go below just yet.

"The storm's on the Cathe now!" Elaine shouted, pointing. In the direction of Thirnmar the clouds were much darker. It was there that the lightning stabbed most frequently, illuminating the clouds from the inside. "Be here soon enough," she predicted.

"A ship!" Lydia shouted suddenly. "No, two! Oh, my, look!"

"Where?" two voices asked. Three pairs of eyes strained in the darkness but it was only when the lightning flashed again that they caught the briefest of glimpses.

Two small ships, not unlike the one that had saluted their tower earlier, were fighting through mountainous seas in the thick of the storm. The rearmost of the two seemed to be having the worst of it. Only one sail was set -a reefed topsail- but through the telescope which was hastily handed around, shredded sails could be seen on other spars.

At one point the troubled vessel took a direct lightning strike to the mainmast but still she battled on; sailing it seemed in company with the other. They were only visible for a short while. The storm front moved on towards Fain-Arn and the heavy rain hid them from view. Their last glimpse was of both ships heeling heavily at the approach of a monstrous wave. The weather closed in before the inevitably gruesome conclusion could be played out.

"What on earth are they doing out there?" Sasha exclaimed, her voice ringing with the shock they all felt. Then: "They may have survived that wave! Elaine, sound the horn for a while; for half an hour at least. If they are still out there, they'll need to keep well clear to stand any chance at all. I'm going down to feed David now. You'll be alright for a while, Lydia?"

"Of course!" The Sheldons went below, leaving a D'Shan on watch. It was a strange situation, Lydia thought as she tried to take her mind off the wet and the cold. She'd have never believed it possible two weeks ago at school that she'd find herself up here in a storm such as this. What, she wondered, would the next two weeks bring? A miracle to save my family's fortune and reputation? Or social disgrace?

The horn sounded below her loud and clear despite the wind, though not half as loud as it was standing next to it. Elaine was well practiced and was able to judge the blasts precisely with just the right amount of time between soundings. Lydia kept a good lookout all around but she kept coming back to the Wes side of the tower in the hope of seeing one or both of the ships. As the horn continued to sound at intervals, the storm's front moved closer. Not once did Lydia see anything of the two ships.

The storm's arrival was announced twenty minutes later in two ways; first by the abrupt change from rain to stinging hail, second by three rapid stabs of lightening and an almost instantaneous thunderclap which shook TolSor to its foundations. This so startled Elaine that the horn fell abruptly silent. Lydia ducked instinctively from the light and noise before cautiously poking her head over the stonework. She was just in time to see a spectacular lightning strike on one of the abandoned towers about four miles away. Something else caught her eye, however. There was movement close by the tower. She stood and ran over to the opposite side. Five figures, one of which was pulling a handcart were approaching TolSor. Another more distant flash revealed muskets in their hands.

Lydia turned and threw herself at the door to the stairway. She ran down so quickly that she lost her footing and arrived in the mechanism room headfirst, falling heavily onto her knees amid a cloud of dust. Her entrance was sufficiently impressive to interrupt Elaine's second attempt to sound the foghorn.

"They're here!" Lydia said urgently. "Five of them, with muskets." Elaine's face paled slightly but she remained her usual decisive self.

"Downstairs!" They pounded down as fast as they could and burst breathlessly into the kitchen where David had just finished his feed. He burped contentedly at them by way of welcome. "Trouble," Elaine announced. "Lydia's seen five men, close by. They're armed."

"Lydia, take David upstairs and tell Dan," Sasha ordered, handing the baby over gently. "There's nothing he can do but he'll want to know what's afoot. Then go back up top and keep an eye on things. Try not to let them see you though. We'll hold the fort down here."

"Yes, Aunt Sasha." Lydia turned and made her way back up the stairs. She had lost count now of the number of times she had climbed and descended the stairs over the past hours. Though her heart pounded, she wasted no time in reaching the second floor. Events were moving fast and all fatigue had fallen away from her to be replaced by a terrible fear which she fought to keep under control.

It occurred to Lydia as she entered the bedroom that this was her first meeting with Elaine's father. He smiled politely as she carefully tucked the gurgling baby into his crib. Then she turned towards the bed. Each quickly summed the other up, assessing what was before them against their preconceptions and prejudices.

Lydia could see that under normal circumstances Dan Sheldon was an imposing man, larger in stature than her father. His present condition was an unwelcome reminder of her own father's appearance the last time she had seen him. The main difference, she quickly decided, was around the eyes. The lines around her father's eyes were generally due to close reading work. Dan's face was weathered and the lines around his eyes were due to squinting in the sun and laughter. His was a face designed to wear a smile, she thought, which must make his present state all the harder for her cousin to bear. Lydia quickly decided that her uncle was a man she could like.

Dan looked for the snobbish arrogance he associated with the D'Shan family but saw instead a girl on the edge of womanhood whose intelligent eyes met his own steadily and whose face softened slightly in genuine sympathy. She was both shorter and slighter than Elaine as well as being very fair-skinned. These were the marks of a wealthy child unaccustomed to labour. However, he sensed strength within her not measured by how heavy a rope she could pull. He remembered Elaine's words, which had troubled him somewhat on reflection: "she's put herself at risk for me once already…" What sort of "risk" had Lydia taken for his daughter he wondered.

"Uncle Daniel, Aunt Sasha wanted you to know. There's five men outside. They're armed. Aunt Sasha and Elaine are downstairs with the muskets. I'm to go upstairs and keep an eye on them from there."

"Five?" Dan tried once again to move but his strength reserves were far too depleted for that. "Damnation!" he cursed as pain racked his body. His sudden pallor and shortness of breath quite alarmed Lydia. Impulsively, she reached out to him. "Easy! You must rest, Uncle. The door is well barred, they won't get in. It's wild out. I can't see them sticking around but if they do we're ready for them. I'll try to let you know what's happening, all right? I know it's hard not knowing. I'd better go."

"Thanks," Dan said weakly. "Take care, lass."

"Always!" Lydia assured him with a smile that was just a little forced. In truth, fear was beginning to take hold but she wasn't about to show it to anyone, least of all her uncle who needed to think everything was well under control. She turned and made her way back up the stairs.

"Brave girl!" Dan muttered to himself. That forced smile had been most revealing. Clearly Lydia was not ignorant of their danger but was concealing her fear as well as she could.

It was indeed wild outside, Lydia discovered. The storm was well and truly upon them now. The wind gusted fiercely. Hail mixed with rain fell relentlessly as the wind and pounding surf combined to assault her ears. Ducking low, Lydia moved to the parapet at the front of the tower and cautiously raised her head. One of the men was looking up, right at her, but she quickly realised he couldn't see her. The falling rain and hail half blinded him and her head was as close to the level of the parapet as possible. The other men appeared to be banging and kicking at the door. Much good may it do you, Lydia thought, remembering the heavy crates behind it. So far, everything appeared to be well under control.

Inside the tower things appeared less certain. Lydia had scarcely left them when the first heavy blow fell on the door. This was accompanied by muffled shouts along the lines of "open up or else" which Elaine and her mother did not dignify with a response. This was followed by a spate of increasingly frenzied thuds and crashes. When one of the men fired his musket at the lock, the ladies of TolSor decided that enough was enough.

Either side of the door was a circular wooden plug. Elaine and her mother carefully removed these to reveal small bore holes which angled out through the wall to emerge outside beside the door. Barely visible from the outside, these bore holes were just about large enough to take the muzzle of a musket. They wedged their guns in place and on a nod from Sasha pulled the triggers together.

The effect on the outside was quite dramatic. The wall spat out two ugly gouts of flame and smoke billowed obscuring the door. A shrill cry indicated that one of the musket balls had found a target. The main effect, as desired, was to cause a hasty retreat from the doorway. Sasha took up the third musket and held it in place, ready to unleash a second shot if they approached the door again. Elaine began to frantically reload the two muskets. As it turned out, she needn't have rushed.

Lydia couldn't see the doorway or the recess from her vantage point without leaning out a good deal further and that was something she wasn't about to contemplate. She saw a curious orange flash but the sound was lost in the wind. She did see four men move very hastily away from the door, one of them clutching his arm. Lydia had discovered that the telescope worked quite well pointing downwards, since the rain couldn't fall on the lens that way. She used this to her advantage, observing through the telescope whilst keeping herself hidden. A conveniently close flash of lightening allowed her to see the blood welling from an ugly upper arm wound. Good. Lydia felt no sympathy at all for the attackers.

They regrouped by the handcart and appeared to have a lively discussion. One figure gestured at the cart but the injured man shook his head and instead waved back at the building. A short heated debate followed before they moved off again; two around the back, two around the front. The injured man remained behind.

"Damn you," Lydia muttered in what was a rare use of strong language. "Now what? Why don't you just clear off home?" She moved stealthily across the tower to see what the pair behind the building were up to. Whatever it was, it was somewhere she couldn't see without risking being seen herself. She strained her ears to catch anything over the noise of the storm which might tell her where to look.

A faint sound reached her ears over by the house but was impossible to identify. "Blast it!" Lydia's nerves were strained and for all her breeding she had a good repertoire of the milder sort of profanity. She stood up. Treacherously, a stab of lightening back-lit her for all the world to see but the men were not looking her way. They had smashed two windows, one to the master bedroom and one to Elaine's room. Two objects were tossed in and they backed away a short distance. They didn't look up or around but stayed fixed on the windows. It took Lydia a while to realise the significance. "No! Oh, heavens, no!" An orange glow flickered on their faces and the first wisps of smoke were snatched out into the night.

At that moment Lydia would have given a good deal for one of the muskets, so filled was she with rage. Instead she turned and ran for the stairs. It never occurred to her to check what had become of the two at the front of the house.

In the tower the tension was palpable. Both Sasha's and Elaine's nerves were on a fine edge, acutely aware of the slightest sound or movement. It was quiet outside after the initial volley but both expected some sort of retaliation. Elaine was reloading the second musket at the table when she thought she heard a noise beyond the door leading to the house. She moved quickly across and pressed her ear to the door (avoiding going anywhere near the lock). She heard a faint crash of breaking glass but that was all.

"I think they're going for the house," she said.

"Trying to draw us out," Sasha replied grimly. "Be ready over there, Elaine. They might try both doors at once. We'll show them we can handle that." The house door also had musket holes beside it. Elaine finished work on the second musket and left it on the table, where either of them could get it, and took up position by the second door. After a lengthy and tense wait it was Elaine's mother who heard something first.

Sasha heard movement shortly before something struck the door with a terrific thump. CRACK! The musket leaped in her hand and again fire and death reached out from the tower. Sasha rushed to the table and snatched up the second musket, leaving the other one to be reloaded.

Unknown to her, the men outside had been waiting for that opportunity. They knew there were only a few defenders with a limited supply of muskets. Each knew pretty well the time it took to reload one and so they had a good idea for how long the door could be approached between shots. An obvious choice for them would have been to try to block the holes but that might entail the loss of life, or a hand, and they were in no mood to take that kind of chance. They had come well equipped, having scouted the tower out in advance.

While Sasha switched muskets, two men dived into the recess and placed a small barrel next to the door before retreating hastily. It would have been better to have laid a proper fuse but that could take a fatally long time. Instead, the top of the barrel was slightly open. It just remained for one man to hurl an oil lantern at the stonework to complete the task. He did so just as Sasha regained her position and Lydia entered the kitchen a short distance away from the door.

The explosion tore the door from its hinges and shredded the first layer of crates to matchwood. The force of the blast was largely absorbed by the barricade but Sasha was too close to miss it entirely. Heat seared her face and arms and she staggered back into the room with a scream. It was the crates which did the most damage. Splinters of wood, large and small, filled the confined space with shrapnel from which no one escaped entirely.

Elaine was furthest away and suffered only mild cuts. Lydia felt a sharp pain in her leg as a large piece of wood sliced past her. Instinctively she threw up her arms to protect her face. The pain was incredible, as if a giant piece of sandpaper had been dragged across her skin. Fortunately, the splinters came from the lighter crates, rather than the more solid door, but they were too numerous to guess at. The pain made her stagger.

Sasha was the least fortunate. As well as being close enough to suffer burns to her face and arms, she was struck by three large splinters. One cracked two ribs and the second broke her left leg just below the knee. The last, mercifully perhaps, knocked her unconscious.

The plan had been for the door to blow inwards followed quickly by the men who had regrouped whilst the fire in the house took hold. The barricade ruined that plan. For a start, the crate with the weight inside hadn't budged. It now presented an obstacle as daunting as the door had been; given that piled in front of it was a formidable mound of debris, most of which had sharp points or edges. Secondly, some of the force of the explosion had been directed out - certainly not part of the plan- and they had been forced to retreat well away while the smoke cleared. Thus the attackers lost their only opportunity to gain entry unopposed.

The house was now well alight. Smoke was pouring from every window and from between the slate tiles. Accessing the tower's inner door was impossible. They had no option but to press ahead with a frontal assault. Urged on by the shouted curses of their injured leader, four men moved up to the tower in a tight bunch. As they clambered up the pile of debris fate, or perhaps some other force, decided to take a hand.

Fain-Arn was virtually in the centre of the storm now. It was raining and hailing so hard that it was questionable whether the men's muskets would actually fire. As the attackers reached a point from which they could aim into the room, lightning struck TolSor. It struck the roof of the lamp room shattering the windows and quenching the lamp. The designers had known this was a possibility and so the tower was liberally fitted with conductors.

Blue fire arced across the top of the tower and down the side. On reaching ground level it earthed via the body of the injured man who was sheltering in the lee of the tower and leaning against the conductor. Death was instantaneous.

In the aftermath of the gunpowder blast, time seemed to slow for those inside the tower. Elaine assumed her mother was dead. It seemed inconceivable that she could have survived the explosion. Not wanting to look at her mother's still body, Elaine looked elsewhere and noticed with horror that Lydia had chosen the worst possible moment to come down the stairs. Her arms were red with blood and she seemed to have trouble putting weight on her left leg but she was nonetheless staggering towards the kitchen table.

"Bloody hellfire!" Elaine had never heard her cousin swear and was too shocked by the moment to realise that she had picked it up from her. "Damn it hurts!" Lydia's eyes were welling with tears as she collapsed onto the bench. Her hands were trembling as they reached for the spare musket on the table. "Watch the door, they'll try something in a minute!"

"Lydia..." Elaine began.

"I'm fine. Those creeps aren't getting in, Elaine. Watch the door." Elaine darted forward and picked up her mother's unfired musket. Her stomach heaved at the sensation of blood on the stock, her mother's blood, but she didn't falter and in a few seconds she was kneeling next to Lydia one musket level, another by her side as Lydia's hands fumbled with the powder horn. Smoke still swirled, unable to clear, and Elaine worried that she wouldn't see their attackers until it was too late. She needn't have done.

The next lightning strike back-lit four torsos atop the barricade. Their muskets were up, but they didn't yet know where to look. CRACK! Elaine gave them a clue. Her musket flashed and leaped in her hands. Rage and grief made her aim deadly accurate. One of the figures abruptly disappeared.

Only one of the three muskets fired in reply. The rest had damp powder. It was an ill-aimed shot which ricocheted off the stone floor and struck Lydia close to the collar bone. It tore through skin but nothing else. So engrossed was she in loading the third musket (her hands, slick with blood, fumbled with the small musket ball unable to pick it up) that she hardly noticed. It was as if her mind had become detached from such matters. She was fairly sure she was going to die but if so it would be after she had handed this loaded musket to her cousin.

Cursing, the men cast their guns aside and drew sabres instead. They began to move over the final crate but the sharp debris snagged their clothes, hampering their efforts. One man's foot slipped between the crate and a mass of iron. It twisted his ankle violently. He dropped the sword and clasped his leg in agony.

Two men finally gained the floor opposite the girls. Their opponents looked anything but fearsome, cowering as they were by the back wall. They knew that one of the girls had just killed their companion with a lucky shot. That was enough to warrant their deaths. They moved quickly, lifting their sabres in readiness.

Time slowed still further. Elaine's second musket fired and at point blank range the outcome was instantly fatal. She dropped the gun and reached for the third but her hands closed on emptiness. Lydia was simply too slow. The second man registered the musket shot and in that split second decided Elaine was the greater threat. He bore down on her, swinging the sabre viciously. In an instant, Elaine recognised the features of the man who had threatened her earlier. She experienced a searing pain down her left side before feeling a crushing weight strike her and drive the breath from her lungs. Her head struck something hard and her hearing faded out as she drifted from consciousness. She had the brief impression of a bright light before the darkness engulfed her.

Lydia's ears were ringing. In her haste and clumsiness, she had heavily over-primed the pan. She had flash burns to the side of her face. In a state of some shock she carefully rested the musket on the table and, ignoring the moans of pain from the man wedged atop their barricade, reached down and with all her strength hauled the dead man off her cousin.

Elaine was still.

"NO!" This was one shock too many and Lydia screamed the word, all the rage and pain tearing from her lungs. Her leg wouldn't bear her weight so she fell ungracefully from the bench to the floor next to Elaine. Sobbing uncontrollably, she cradled her friend's head in her arms as her grief poured out. It took some time to realise that Elaine was still warm; more than that, there appeared to be no blood. The man had stumbled at the last minute as he tried to evade the shot from the musket in Lydia's hands. The hilt of his sabre had struck Elaine just below the ribs as he fell, but the blade had missed and shattered on the stone floor. "Elaine? Elaine! Wake up!" Lydia brought her face close to her friend's mouth – her ears were still deafened from the musket blast. It took an age, but she eventually detected the faintest of breaths. "You'll be all right," Lydia promised, resting her friend's head gently down onto her lap. "I'm right here with you."

Chapter Twelve - The Clouds Clear

The smoke from TolSor's longhouse was visible for miles in the dull light of the morning beneath still-dark clouds and squally rain showers. Several people took note and by ten o'clock the first of them arrived to a scene of shocking devastation.

Edward clambered up the debris and found himself looking down the barrel of a musket in Lydia's determined hands. Her appearance was wild. Her clothes were torn and bloodied. Her face was blackened from the musket blast while her eyes were red and raw from crying and lack of sleep. She shared the room with two corpses and two severely concussed relatives. Edward had passed two other bodies on his way in. The sprained-ankle man had long since made his escape.

"Alright, lass. You remember me, from The Mermaid? I'm a friend of the family. Where's Dan and the baby?"

"Upstairs," Lydia nodded her head. "I couldn't go up though the baby's been crying. My leg's not too good."

"You'll be fine now, lass. There's more help on the way. It's over now. You can put the gun down. You've done enough." Slowly, the musket lowered to the floor. Only when he was sure Lydia didn't see him as a threat did Edward enter the room. "Will you be alright here for a moment longer? I'll wager Dan's going out of his mind up there!"

Edward's visit upstairs was very brief indeed. Just long enough to say that everyone was alive though, yes, they were hurt and to tell Dan he'd have to look after the baby a while longer. In less than two minutes he was back and looking after the injured.

In his years at sea, Edward had seen a fair few head injuries. He quickly decided that neither one was fatal. Both Sasha and Elaine were lucid enough, though they'd had the sort of night that could turn the wits of anyone. Similarly, cuts, grazes and shot wounds were nothing new. By the time the first of the militia from Perth Cathe arrived, Lydia's wounds had been dressed navy fashion with clean sheets from the bunks upstairs. The militiaman turned out to be the next of many visitors that day.

The men who came were mostly fishermen from Perth Cathe. They regarded Dan as one of their own despite his "other job" as tower keeper. For the rest of the day they treated the women of the tower like royalty. Neither girl was permitted to stir from their place at the table close to the roaring fire. Sasha's leg was set by Edward and secured with a splint. This prevented her from being able to move at all; particularly once a very hungry baby was brought to her. While some of the men attended to the tower itself, others set about searching the ruined house for anything salvageable. The heavy crate, which had probably saved their lives, now saved them from awkward questions. Edward and another man discreetly moved it back over the trap door.

At about one o'clock, the coach belonging to Math Forngarth pulled up. Eleanor herself descended from the coach to survey the scene with obvious horror. By this time the team of twelve men had made some impact on things. The bodies were decently covered and removed from the immediate area. Debris from the doorway was cleared away behind the tower out of sight. The interior had been thoroughly swept, mopped and swept again. The business of TolSor, even down to the winding of the weights, had also been taken care of. When Eleanor entered the kitchen she was immediately offered a seat by Edward who had installed himself as housekeeper for the day.

"Hello Mother," Sasha smiled nervously. "No real harm done, we're all here to tell the tale." It proved to be quite some tale. Sasha was understandably hazy about much of the night's events so it fell to the girls to fill in the gaps. Eleanor listened impassively, well accustomed to hiding her real feelings. Edward found himself unable not to listen, though he managed to do so fairly discretely.

"You, David and the girls must come to Forngarth, tonight," Eleanor said. That was not to be. Sasha was not about to leave Dan, who was too weak to make such a journey and the girls were unwilling to leave Sasha. In any case Sasha's leg would not take kindly to the rough ride in a coach. Eleanor wisely let the matter drop. "Very well," she said when the debate eventually reached its conclusion. "I shall send word to your father immediately, Lydia, so that he knows you are well. Rumour travels quickly about the island and we would not want him to think you have come to harm. You will not be alone tonight I trust?"

"No, ma'am they shall not," Edward confirmed. "Never you fear. I shall keep good watch tonight as will a few others."

"That is for the best," Eleanor agreed. "Very well. Take care all of you. I do not want to be in the way…" she raised her hand and smiled at the chorus of protest. "You are very kind but you have help of a practical sort which is what you need most for now. I will serve you better by returning when your immediate need has passed and our thoughts turn to the future. You have, I think, earned yourselves the right to some peace and quiet. I can see you are in good hands." She stood to leave but turned back and addressed the girls directly.

"You did very well, girls, both of you. Exceptionally well." With those words she took her leave. Sasha smiled and squeezed her daughter's hand.

Eleanor had not long departed when there came a shout from outside the tower. Despite Edward's entreaties Elaine could not be prevented from rushing to the door to see what was afoot. She stood in the doorway for a moment then turned to Lydia who was unable to move.

"It's a ship, two-master. They're hove-to just off the entrance to the cov and they're lowering a boat. Looks like they've been through it - foretopmast is gone, mainyards sprung by the look of it on the fore and main. Lost most of the bowsprit too. They've just a short stump left. There's a tattered staysail and main topsail set. I'm not sure how they're managing to hold station in this swell. They must be holed below the waterline too - there's a fair fountain of water being pumped out over the bows. I wonder why they've stopped here? It's a shipyard they need - unless they saw the smoke from the house." Elaine turned, making her head swim. She reached out to the wall to steady herself. "All right, I'll sit back down now Edward! You can stop looking at me like that as well Lydia! You look a fright too you know!" The girls traded a rueful smile.

"I'll be back in a while," Edward told them. "I don't know what these gents are about but I'll send 'um packing. We've enough to deal with here." He checked the pistol in his belt, grabbed a musket then headed down to the cov. He was gone some time. When he returned he was not alone.

"Master Berant!" the girls called out together, recognising the robed figure they had last seen at Wescliffe.

"May I come in?" he asked, pausing at the doorway and looking directly at Sasha.

"Of course. I am sorry we cannot welcome you as you deserve." Sasha made an effort to move towards the fire and the kettle but blanched as pain shot up her leg.

"Be still, I beg." Master Berant moved hastily in from the doorway. He rested a hand on her arm in a reassuring gesture. "Let the guest attend the host just this once." He turned to the fireplace. "The tea is in this tin? Ah, yes!" He busied himself, insisting on making tea for everyone including Edward who, though utterly overawed, accepted it gladly. After a few minutes they were all sat companionably around the table together.

"A bad blow last night," Edward offered, lest there be an awkward silence.

"Yes, is your ship badly damaged? Did you get caught in it?" Elaine's questions tumbled out in a rush.

"Hush now," Edward rebuked sharply. "A Weatherworker doesn't get caught by a storm. Fancy saying such a thing, Miss Elaine!" Elaine blushed and looked down into her mug but Daren laughed heartily.

"No more he does, master Edward, yet we were in the worst of it nonetheless. No, Elaine, my ship has suffered but not as badly as some. She'll carry me to the yards. Once we have repaired I shall be leaving for Forath. My work here is complete. It was a bad blow as you say - the worst this island has had for some time I fancy. It was not altogether a natural occurrence. Whilst you had your troubles here, an altogether darker struggle was playing out offshore."

"This sounds like a tale!" Edward was forgetting his reserve as his curiosity was piqued.

"Yes, do tell us!" It was Lydia who spoke. Elaine's eyes sparked with curiosity too.

"Very well. I do so because this concerns you and it is right that you should hear. But this tale does not go beyond these walls. It is not for every ear that I speak." Daren Berant could be very stern when he chose to be and this command rang with authority. He looked at each of them for assent before he continued.

"My first order of business after we met last was to convey your mother to Thirnmar, Lydia. We had a good crossing and I was able to set her ashore at Perth Laird on the morning after we left Wescliffe. I believe she has a cousin in the city who she intends to stay with for the time being. She said your father would have the address. She was quite well when I left her." Lydia smiled, grateful that her unasked question had been answered.

"I then returned to Perth Calran since there was the matter of your cousin Tristan to be resolved. We didn't arrive until late that evening and there was little for me to do until the following day when I called on the Governor. I must say, young Tristan had been busy! He had fairly terrorised the Governor's household and I had no doubt he would also call at Forngarth, though my mind was easy on that score." The girls both smiled, recalling the manner of Tristan's departure from Forngarth. "My concern was what his next move would be. Having lost you, Lydia, as leverage against the family and having not the power or character to subdue your Grandmother, Elaine, it seemed most probable to me that he would leave the island and attempt some mischief over on Thirnmar.

We therefore put to sea that night and set ourselves the task of watching the Cathe. I had checked both Perth Calran and Perth Cathe thoroughly of course, so it seemed likely that his ship would be on the other side of the island at Cov Nor. We kept watch upon the waters to the nor-est.

The first day we saw nothing. Nor for much of the second but in the middle part of that afternoon we sighted a vessel attempting to slip along the coast close inshore. We moved to intercept and so the duel began." Daren paused and looked around the table. He had their complete attention.

"Let me just say that you are never to underestimate the threat a Void Mage such as Tristan poses. Their power is no different to those of us trained at the Kerun Dur who use the Gift but their application is much different. They have no compunction about destroying anything or anyone who stands in their way. Tristan knew I was a match for him and so he declined to face me immediately. We began a game of cat and mouse that was to last the rest of the day, all that night and much of the following day too.

His ship would feint and turn away if we spotted it. He tried to draw us onto the rocks, creating powerful currents that would grip the keel and which required all of my Art to pull us free from again. For each blow he made I was forced to offer a counterstroke. In my pride, I thought perhaps I would best him there and then. I hoped that he would turn and run. Alas for my folly! He was gaining my measure with each test. With each counter his malice grew. Finally, he unleashed a terrible wave upon us that drove my ship onto its beam ends and destroyed much rigging as well as those sails that we had set. By the time we had righted ourselves, he had slipped by and was heading out into the Cathe.

Only then did I perceive the true measure of our opponent, for the sky away to the Sor-Wes was darkening with an approaching storm that was of his making. It was his intention to command the storm and use it as cover for his escape."

"Surely, he cannot have thought that would serve against a Weatherworker?" Edward burst out.

"And why not, master Edward? He is born of this world and his soul is tied to water. The void can command as ably as the light. The sea is both a destructive and life-giving element. It is as much his to command as it is mine." Daren paused to allow that lesson to sink in before continuing.

"The direction of the wind made it hard for us from the start. We had to make good the damage before we could set any sails. Tristan had been a bit too eager and the wind made his own life difficult too. Because of this we did not fall too far behind our quarry. We chased him down the Cathe into the evening. All the while the seas and wind grew more dangerous. I did what I could to protect my ship from the worst of it but I cannot say I have ever faced such fury at sea. Finally, as the storm's grip tightened upon us we closed with our quarry and the duel began in earnest.

He called down strike after strike of lightning onto my ship, and threw such waves our way that the bowsprit was rent in half. In return, I was able to command waves of my own, and currents too, that gave him plenty to worry about in such seas."

"We saw you!" Elaine exclaimed suddenly. "Two ships, out on the Cathe, that was before the storm properly reached us and the men came. I thought both ships must have been broached - we saw a massive wave."

"Indeed." Daren's face darkened with the recollection. "So reckless was Tristan in his anger that I believe he vowed to destroy me even if it meant his own life. He tore a rent in the sea, as deep as the ocean floor itself, and forced it into a deadly wave. Had it not been countered it would have destroyed much of the island's Wes coast and all of the shipping in Perth Cathe."

"How did you counter such a thing as that?" Edward asked incredulously. He had heard many a tall sea-tale in The Mermaid but none as vivid and dark as this.

"I did not." Daren replied quietly. "I have not the power or Art to do so. In disturbing the depths, Tristan awoke one of the greatest powers in our world. A Neriad." There was a collective gasp from around the table. Each of them knew of Neriads as myth. The powerful spirits of the sea were said to guard and control their element. If not appeased, or if angered, their displeasure was said to be inescapable doom for any seafarer. Conversely, their gift upon those they favoured was said to be safety in even the most appalling storm.

"It was the Neriad that saved my ship, though even she could not prevent some damage to our hull. We also lost yet more sails and spars when the wave struck us. When the maelstrom passed we found we had been carried far beyond Elledran. The sea was so rough even there that only now have we limped back to make landfall."

"What happened to...?" Elaine's question hung in the air.

"I cannot say. Tristan's ship was most certainly destroyed and all aboard her drowned. The Neriad took hold of it in her anger and drew it down into the depths with her. The Void Mages are said to be protected from death, until such a time as their power is spent when the void claims them. It may be his time came, or he may have escaped back to the Dark Peak on Erath where the Die Kashaan Eed have their tower. Only time will tell. He will not return here, however, of that you can be sure. The Neriad would never permit him passage. The seas around Thirnmar are forever closed to him." Master Berant fell silent. Those around the table were quiet too, each with their own thoughts.

Lydia's thoughts were of her cousin and the dark menace he had carried with him when he had confronted her and Elaine on the heath near to Wescliffe. Master Berant's news brought a relief from that threat which had been present in the back of her mind since that day.

Elaine's sombre thoughts were with the hapless crew of Tristan's ship, as were Edward's. Loss at sea was something every seafaring family faced but it was never an easy thing to be confronted with, whatever the circumstances. There was also the unspoken message in Master Berant's tale, that the seas about their shores were guarded and influenced by the most ancient and formidable of forces. This, surely, must be part of the secret Master Berant wished them to keep. Each person around the table knew they would never feel quite the same again when out on the water. Master Berant rose to his feet.

"Mrs Sheldon, with your permission, I have talked long enough. Pray allow me to attend to your wounds and those of the girls. Once I have done so I shall see what can be done for your husband."

Light was fading in the late afternoon before Daren Berant took his leave. He left the patients in a much better state than at his arrival; though even his Art could not do much to speed the process of healing cracked ribs and broken bones. He had done much to make the healing process more comfortable and there would be no infection. Healing water applied with poultices and administered in small doses as a drink would see to that. Edward saw Master Berant down to the wharf. Before he descended to the boat, Daren asked a favour of him.

"Please see that this letter is delivered to Forngarth. And keep a good watch until you hear that the threat to the girls has passed. I judge that it will not be too long, one way or another."

"Very good, Master I shall see it delivered." Edward touched his cap respectfully. "Never you fear, sir. They'll meet a reception too warm for their liking if they return here again. Good fortune be with you, Master."

"Fair winds and safe return." Daren nodded to the crew. They pushed away from the jetty then began to row back out to the ship. The boat was aided by a helpful current that carried it easily and safely past the rocks at the Cov entrance. Once he saw they were clear, Edward returned to TolSor. His first act was to dispatch a mounted militiaman to Forngarth with the letter. His second was to check that no-one would be able to approach the tower from any side without being challenged. Only then did he return inside to try to ensure the owners went to bed to get some much-needed rest.

That evening, at Edward's insistence, the family retired early. Fatigue had at last caught up with all of them. There were two men on the roof and Edward in the kitchen with three loaded muskets by his side. The family knew they could sleep soundly. For the first time in a very long time, Sasha tucked her daughter in and kissed her goodnight, experiencing a twinge of pain as she did so.

"Goodnight Mother, I love you," Elaine responded, just as she had when she was younger. The words somehow carried more meaning now. On reflection, Sasha did the same for Lydia who of the two was still in the most pain, though not mentioning it at all.

"Goodnight, Aunt Sasha."

"Sleep well, my dear," Sasha replied. "And thank you, for everything. We'd not have made it without you."

"Family..." Lydia murmured, drifting off to sleep.

"Family," Sasha repeated softly and limped across to her own bed, thinking that as a group they were in a bit of a state. It has certainly come to something, she reflected with a bitter smile, if the healthiest member of the household is the baby!

Outside, in the fading light, Groth watched the activity around the tower. How could those fools have failed? He raged to himself. Now I've no goods and the girls are well guarded. What can I do? How do I get out of this? There was only one answer to that. A desperate one, true, but he was now short of options. He returned to his horse and galloped back towards Perth Cathe, though that was not his intended destination.

Chapter Thirteen - Endings and Beginnings

The arrival at Wescliffe of Eleanor D'Shan's terse letter was very welcome. It was placed in Thomas's hand a scant hour after the first rumour had reached him that TolSor had been raised to the ground by an unidentified group of bandits. Thomas D'Shan had been given much time to think, and to regain his strength, since the girls' departure. His health was much improved but his position was not.

Ruin faced him and he had come to terms with the fact. It would mean a move, probably to Thirnmar, but the family name would prevent him falling too far. In all honesty he had no appetite now for Wescliffe or his job. Nothing was worth the worry of the hour preceding Eleanor's note when he had imagined his only child dead. It was time to cut his losses. There was only one matter remaining to be resolved and it was by no means a small one. Little honour was left to him, Thomas knew, but there was one aspect of his personal code that no-man should violate except at risk of his life. It had been violated and now it was time to deal with that. Thomas had a pretty good idea how things might go now. It was just a matter of planning and trusting to luck. Unfortunately, his luck had been noticeably absent of late.

Master Berant's advice had been well heeded since his departure. Wescliffe was guarded at night with at least two members of the household awake and alert at all times. The attack on TolSor prompted a further beefing up of these arrangements and Thomas himself decided to remain awake; the better to assist his servants when the time came. He had no doubt that he would be called upon this night.

It was hardly unexpected, but annoying nonetheless. Groth could see lights burning inside Wescliffe. Shadows moved inside and outside the house. This was going to be very difficult. Waiting a day or so would make it easier but Jewkes' deadline was fast approaching and it was not one he could afford to miss. Luckily, Groth had been keeping a very close eye on Wescliffe and knew of a weakness in the defences. It lay in the fact that one of the stable-hands was a bit partial to a drink, as a result of which he never made it all the way through his watch without nodding off. Patience was all that was required. Patience and a steady nerve.

When the time came, Groth was fully ready. He slipped by the open stable, from which snoring was emanating, and moved stealthily to a point where he could climb up onto the roof. Entering the deserted servant's quarters was easy – the window latches were child's play to defeat - and from there he could enter the heart of the house via the servant's corridor. Timing got tricky then. There were people patrolling the yard who might hear or see him but he knew the house and its hiding places well enough. Finally, he slipped into Thomas's study undetected.

Thomas was at his desk sprawled over his papers fast asleep. One arm rested beneath his head the other hung down at his side. A pistol rested on the desk beside his head. It was all Groth could do not to laugh out loud. He pocketed Thomas's pistol before jabbing him sharply in the temple with his own. With a startled grunt the man awoke, reaching for a pistol that wasn't there.

"Evening, Thomas," Groth said pleasantly. "Don't call out, that would be a needless waste of your life, don't you think?"

"What do you want now, Groth?" Thomas' voice was weary.

"Simply money, I'm afraid," Groth answered. "You will, if you please, write a note drawing on the Revenue Account for the sum of three hundred crowns. I am quite prepared to shoot you, and any other members of your household, then forge the note myself. However, I feel our long standing business partnership requires that I give you the chance to live."

"You are generous to a fault," hate sounded in Thomas' voice but he had already decided how he would deal with this situation should luck fail him yet again. He reached for a piece of paper and wrote the required note, signing with a flourish that almost broke the nib of his pen. "Your money. May I say you really are the most contemptible man I have ever met?"" Groth smiled.

"You may. I take such words as compliments. Thank you, Thomas. Now, one last thing. You see, I am only too aware that you can rescind this note as easily as you wrote it."

"Why would I do that?" Thomas asked quickly; fear ringing in his voice as he saw the inevitable road Groth's logic was taking.

"You are a petty man, Thomas, and unfortunately you are not quite up to your end of the business partnership. With regret, I shall have to end it." Groth moved back to the door, covering Thomas carefully. Thomas's shoulders sagged in final defeat. Groth could not resist pausing to savour the moment. "Goodbye, Thomas." His attention focussed on the man's face, his expression of defeat and fear, turning to... what? It was Groth's last thought. Thomas's left hand had dropped from sight; he was right handed and carefully kept his "dangerous" hand in plain view. Beneath the large desk a shotgun had been fixed in place with brackets. As Groth gloated, Thomas's fingers closed on the trigger. Groth died painfully but far quicker, Thomas thought, than he deserved.

Morning at TolSor brought bright sunlight and the sense that, as a family, they had faced adversity together but not come out too badly. The loss of the house was a grievous blow certainly but houses can be rebuilt. Time had allowed each of them to consider how much more could so easily have been lost. They all greeted the new day with optimism rather than fear or despair.

Edward helped Dan down from the bedroom so that he could spend the day around his family. He then made himself scarce in order that they might have time to talk and begin to laugh again. A strong breed, this lot, Edward mused to himself, settling on some rocks and casting out a line. Few could have weathered events as well.

News arrived from Perth Cathe that evening describing how an intruder at Wescliffe had been shot dead by the Revenue Officer who had caught him trying to steal from the office. Evidently Mr D'Shan himself was unharmed, having taken the precaution of arming himself with a shotgun before challenging the burglar. From the description of the dead man both girls knew that the last of their troubles were over and those too of Elaine's father. This, as much as the healing potion left by Master Berant, did much to set them on the path to recovery.

Gradually, as the days passed, life at the tower settled back into routine. Only Edward stayed on after the militiamen were recalled and the fishermen returned to their boats in Perth Cathe.

First Elaine, then Lydia recovered to the point that they could begin to help operate the tower. They also assisted with the painful job of sifting through the shell of the longhouse; searching for scraps of belongings that could be salvaged.

Dan's wound ceased to fester and began to heal. The deathly pallor and fever passed within a few days of Master Berant's visit. Though the road to full recovery for both he and his wife would be long, there was no doubt that they would both do so in the fullness of time.

Two weeks passed and the first hard frosts of winter were making themselves felt when a letter arrived from Forngarth to say that Eleanor would visit the following day.

Eleanor D'Shan arrived as promised in the early afternoon to find the family laughing together in the kitchen. They looked much healthier than the last time she had seen them. They welcomed her kindly enough, but in a short while a slight awkwardness became apparent. Eleanor decided that it was time to do what she had come to do.

"If you will permit me, Daniel, I have a few things to say to you all." Elaine's father nodded though his eyes became guarded. "It's no secret, Sasha that your father did not approve of your marriage to this fine man. I supported your choice, as you know, but I did not speak out against his decision to cut you off financially." She looked across at Dan. "Am I not right in thinking that Rupert accused you of marrying my daughter for her money?"

"He did," Dan confirmed, his face flushing in anger at the recollection. "I've never given anyone cause to repeat that falsehood. I said I'd marry Sasha without a penny from Forngarth and my word has been proven true!"

"Indeed. You were, I think, manoeuvred into that position rather cruelly. However, I too must share the blame. Rupert has been dead these five years past and I have not attempted to redress the injustice of the situation. I'm not saying that you would have accepted money had it been offered, but the fact is I never made the offer. Instead, you have felt yourself forced to undertake certain activities in order to support my eldest grandchild through her schooling. That is something I am heartily sorry for."

"Mother! We've never asked for anything. You must not blame yourself for any of this!" Sasha reached out and squeezed her mother's hand. Eleanor smiled at her but addressed her granddaughter directly.

"Elaine, dear, one thing you must understand. There is very little in this world that families cannot reach agreement on and very few problems they cannot solve. They fail only when they do not try. The combination of stubbornness on the part of my late husband, pride on the part of your father and stupidity on mine has brought us to this. I am sorry, my girl, deeply sorry. We must now set things to rights.

Daniel, you have been married to my daughter for sixteen years. Your word, as far as my late husband is concerned, has been proved true. Is that not correct?"

Dan thought hard for a moment, suspecting the direction the conversation was going In. He had sworn an oath to love Sasha without a penny of her family's money. However, although he had hitherto regarded that as a lifelong undertaking, he'd never actually said that he'd not take any even if it were offered. Had he fulfilled the promise to the late Admiral? If so, was it time to move on? Stubborn though he was, Eleanor's words were true and he could not deny their logic, or the faint hope they offered. He nodded slowly.

"I'll take that as given," he agreed. "If Sasha feels the same."

"I do," she said quickly, with a loving look. "You're a good husband, Dan Sheldon."

"Very well." Eleanor allowed herself to smile. "I am, you may have noticed, getting on in years. Forngarth is a large estate and I am finding the management of it increasingly difficult. I would like you to come up and live at the house. The estate will pass to you in any case upon my death. I propose to make you manager of the estate until such a time that it passes to you in my will. I beg you to consider this very carefully. We cannot change the past but we should grasp the opportunities that the future offers. There is no question of pride or charity here, though there is more than a little responsibility. Think about it for a moment." Eleanor sighed.

"Now, Elaine. You and Lydia, to whom I shall speak in a moment, have suffered in this business. That, too, is partly my fault as I said earlier. I have written instructions to my accountants that from the beginning of next month they are to credit an account in your name with one sixteenth of Forngarth's income. I leave the matter of a dowry to your parents."

"Thank you, Grandma!" Elaine gave the old lady a rough hug and a kiss. Her parents might choose to refuse their part of the offer but this was made directly to her in kind spirit and she wasn't about to refuse it.

"Lydia D'Shan," Eleanor said finally once Elaine had settled back down. "When we last met, I spoke of the situation with your father. At that time, I felt sympathy for you. Now I find I am in your debt for saving Elaine's life. You held your nerve and did what few others could or would have done under such terrible circumstances. You displayed bravery and degree of family loyalty that cannot be expressed by mere words. Such debts cannot really be repaid, at least not in material terms, but as a start I make this offer:

If you so desire, I shall become your legal guardian. You will have an allowance equal to Elaine's. In addition, provision will be made in terms of a dowry that will permit you to marry for love. If you choose a poor man, you will live comfortably. If you choose a wealthy man, he will find no shame in asking for your hand. Will you accept?"

Lydia's mind raced. Etiquette required a reply along the lines of "I couldn't possibly..." but etiquette was, at times, another word for plain stupidity. What her Great Aunt was offering was a gift beyond what it first seemed. She was offering true financial independence, even after marriage. In short, what she was being offered was nothing less than complete and permanent freedom from the chains Lydia had feared since being sent to Harton School. She would be able to follow her own course in life.

"I accept, Great Aunt. Thank you." Another embrace followed, quite as loving as the first.

"Now, Daniel, what of you?" In the end, all Dan had to do was look to his wife and see the hope in her eyes.

"I accept your offer," he replied. "Thank you, Lady D'Shan." He kissed her hand. Eleanor surprised him by shaking his to seal the agreement in a business-like fashion. The old lady had a grip like a vice.

"One last thing, if you will permit the impertinence," Eleanor said. "In respect of the girls' schooling. If Lydia is to become my ward, I must insist on the best for her and not all of the reports I hear of Harton School are good. I think a change is in order there."

Both girls experienced a sudden sickening feeling. It had all been going far too well. Now, at the last minute, they sensed something bad was about to happen.

"I know of a better establishment where the girls can learn all they need to progress in the world. Entry is, I must confess, somewhat difficult but the learning and effort required to pass the necessary tests are both beneficial in practical terms and in terms of character building."

Oh heavens! Elaine thought to herself. She's planning to send us to one of those schools for the aristocracy. You have to pass an exam just to get in one of those places! How many Mary Newtons will I have to endure in a place like that? But her grandmother's previous offer trapped both girls into accepting whatever their fate might be.

"I have received a letter stating that both girls would be welcome, should they present themselves, at the private school of the Guild of Navigators and Weatherworkers on the island of Forath. They have each been given a bursary covering all expenses for their time there should they accept the offer. I believe that although they are still a little young, the girls have proved themselves sufficiently in these last couple of weeks that we should consider sending them immediately."

For once, and possibly the only time ever, both girls were speechless at the same time. Dan's face broke into a broad grin of pure pride.

"I reckon that's a grand idea!" he said. "What do you say, our lass?"

It took just two days for Lydia's father to sign the document making her a legal ward of her Great Aunt. Wescliffe was being emptied of the family's belongings ready for a new occupant and he was preparing to cross to Thirnmar in disgrace. Eleanor's offer had come as a surprise and despite being sure his wife would oppose the idea, Thomas welcomed the chance to isolate his daughter from further harm.

On a crisp Winter's day a week later, when they might have been passing back into school to catch up with missed studies, Lydia and Elaine instead found themselves aboard SKYLARK. Their belongings were stowed below. Elaine was preparing to raise the anchor and set sail. In Lydia's pocket, safely ensconced beneath a warm coat and a waterproof cloak, was a letter of introduction to the Guild's representative on the nearby island of Nellad. It was from there, they had been told, that their journey would begin in earnest.

"All set?" Dan's voice rang out from the shore.

"Aye!" The girls saw their elderly aunt/grandmother raise her cane. Faintly, they caught the syllables of a language they didn't understand. From nowhere a light off-shore breeze sprang up. Laughing together, the girls set SKYLARK's sails and weighed anchor. Their boat turned smartly in the breeze before moving smoothly out of CovTol.

"Good fortune be with you!" It was Dan's voice again. Elaine raised her own.

"Fair winds and safe return! Goodbye!" They passed quickly out into Carras Sound which was still rougher than normal, though nothing out of the ordinary for the season.

"It feels strange to be leaving Fain-Arn," Lydia remarked as SKYLARK began to ride the swell drenching both girls in the process.

"We'll be back!" Elaine assured her, as they altered course and the waving figures were hidden from view. They travelled in silence for a few moments before a loud sound rang out behind them. TolSor's horn sounded three times, a final farewell from Elaine's parents.

For a moment Elaine passed the helm to Lydia and stood, hanging firmly to the shrouds, gazing back at her former home. She fixed the image in her mind: the dark rocks at the foot of the cliff against which the waves foamed and broke ceaselessly. The tower standing stark, straight and proud against the gloomy overcast sky. Leaving it, and knowing she would never live there again, was a painful wrench despite the excitement of what was to come. Tears streamed down her cheeks and, after one last look, she turned her head forward allowing her tears to dry in the brisk cold wind.

The hardest moment for Lydia came some hours later as they sailed Nor past Wescliffe. She looked; hoping to see her father on the cliff top but no one was there. Tears now welled up in her eyes and she handed the tiller to Elaine, ashamed with herself for being so weak. It never occurred to her that "weak" was a word that Elaine would never associate with her cousin.

Reaching into the pocket of her coat, in hope of finding a handkerchief, Lydia's hand closed instead onto a small envelope. She pulled it out. It was the one her father had given her on the night of their escape. She opened it now. It contained a short note in her mother's writing.

Lydia, This was once given to me; now I give it to you. Wear it and may good fortune always be with you.

Inside the envelope was a ring, carved out of a material Lydia did not recognise. It appeared to be decorated with tiny carved shells. The detail was amazing and clearly the work of a master craftsman. Lydia slipped the ring onto her finger.

"I'll not be seeing the inside of that place again, will I?" she asked, nodding across the water. Elaine shook her head.

"On the whole I think it's for the best, don't you?"

"I suppose," Lydia agreed. "Do you think our lives might quieten down a bit now? This holiday has been, well, eventful but I've had enough adventure for now I think."

"Adventure? That was nothing!" Elaine grinned wickedly. "You just wait! We're joining the Guild of Navigators and Weatherworkers! This isn't the end. It's just the beginning!"

23636011R00075

Printed in Great Britain
by Amazon